The Curious Adventures of Penelope Pine

Freya and Mick Jobe

Published by Freya and Mick Jobe, 2024.

This is a work of fiction. Similarities to real people, places, or events are entirely coincidental.

THE CURIOUS ADVENTURES OF PENELOPE PINE

First edition. October 6, 2024.

Copyright © 2024 Freya and Mick Jobe.

ISBN: 979-8227058287

Written by Freya and Mick Jobe.

The Curious Adventures of Penelope Pine

Penelope Pine was not like most children in her village. While the other children found joy in ordinary games and predictable routines, Penelope's heart longed for something more. She was a girl who never stopped asking questions—about the sky, the wind, the rustling leaves, and the strange shimmering lights she sometimes glimpsed in the forest beyond her home. She wasn't content with simple answers, because Penelope believed, with every fibre of her being, that the world was filled with secrets just waiting to be uncovered.

She lived on the edge of Windy Hollow, a small, peaceful village surrounded by rolling hills and quiet streams. The people of Windy Hollow were content with their simple lives, but Penelope couldn't shake the feeling that the world was bigger—much bigger—than anyone else could see. From her bedroom window, she often watched the forest on the horizon, a place adults spoke of in whispers and passed by with hurried steps. But Penelope's curiosity only grew. It was as if the trees were calling to her, inviting her to discover their mysteries.

One evening, as the sun dipped below the hills and the sky turned a deep violet, Penelope spotted something strange. In the distance, just beyond the forest's edge, a soft glow pulsed like a heartbeat in the darkness. It was faint, barely noticeable, but to Penelope, it was a sign—an invitation to adventure.

And so, without a second thought, she packed a small bag, laced up her boots, and set out into the unknown. Little did she know, this would be the beginning of the most extraordinary adventure she had ever imagined—a journey through enchanted lands, magical creatures, and ancient mysteries that only the bravest of hearts could unlock.

Penelope Pine wasn't just about to explore a forest; she was about to discover a world full of wonders, the kind of wonders that only exist for those bold enough to seek them.

This is the story of that journey—The Curious Adventures of Penelope Pine.

Chapter 1: The Mysterious Forest

Penelope Pine was a girl who never let questions rest. From the moment she could form her first words, her parents quickly learned that nothing in their home would ever go unquestioned. Why is the sky blue? Where do butterflies go at night? What makes the wind whistle? Penelope's curiosity was a force of nature, and though the adults around her tried their best to answer her endless stream of inquiries, Penelope was rarely satisfied. The world, as she saw it, was far too full of wonder to be explained by simple answers.

She lived on the edge of Windy Hollow, a small village tucked between rolling hills and whispering trees. The village was surrounded by meadows, rivers, and farms, but it was the towering line of trees on the distant horizon that always captured Penelope's imagination. The forest—dark, dense, and inviting—loomed like a great mystery waiting to be solved.

Penelope's mother had warned her many times not to go near it.

"Stay away from the forest," her mother would say, shaking her head. "It's a dangerous place. No one knows what's in there, and I'd rather not find out. It's best you stick to the fields and gardens where it's safe."

But Penelope was not the kind of girl who could be kept from the unknown by a few words of caution. Every time she walked to school, she would look longingly at the edge of the forest, wondering what lay beyond the shadows of those towering trees. The other children never paid much attention to it—they were too busy with their games and lessons. But to Penelope, the forest was alive with possibilities.

One afternoon, as the autumn sun began to sink low in the sky, Penelope found herself wandering toward the forest's edge. She hadn't planned on it. In fact, she had simply gone for a walk along the stream near her house, thinking she might collect a few pebbles or watch the fish darting under the water's surface. But as she walked, her feet carried her farther and farther away from the familiar paths. Soon, the fields gave way to tall grass, and the comforting babble of the stream faded behind her. The trees loomed closer, their thick branches reaching out like beckoning fingers.

Penelope stopped for a moment at the very edge of the forest, her heart fluttering with excitement and a tinge of nervousness. The air felt different here—cooler, heavier, and filled with the scent of earth and moss. The leaves rustled overhead, but the sound was different from the wind she was used to hearing in the open meadows. It was softer, almost like a whisper.

She glanced over her shoulder. No one was around. In fact, it felt as if no one had been around for a very long time. The forest had a forgotten quality to it, as if people had simply stopped noticing it existed. Penelope took a deep breath and stepped forward, her foot crunching on a layer of dry leaves.

The moment she crossed into the shadow of the trees, something shifted. It was subtle at first, just a feeling—like the air itself had changed. The world behind her, with its familiar fields and distant village, seemed to fade away. The forest was quiet, too quiet. No birds chirped, no animals scurried in the underbrush. It was as if the whole place was holding its breath, waiting.

Penelope's pulse quickened. She wasn't scared, exactly, but there was a strange energy here, something ancient and watchful. She looked around, taking in her surroundings. The trees were massive, their trunks so wide it would take several people to wrap their arms around one. Their bark was dark and rough, covered in patches of emerald-green moss. The ground was soft beneath her feet, a mixture of damp earth and fallen leaves that muffled her footsteps.

She walked deeper into the forest, her curiosity driving her forward. As she ventured further, she began to notice things—small things, at first. The way the light filtered through the leaves, casting strange, dappled shadows on the ground. The way certain trees seemed to twist in unnatural ways, their branches curling like the fingers of an old hand. And then there was the sound—a low, almost imperceptible hum that seemed to rise and fall with the breeze.

After what felt like only a few minutes, Penelope realized she was no longer sure which way she had come. She turned around, expecting to see the edge of the forest behind her, but all she saw were more trees. They stood silently, as if watching her, their branches swaying ever so slightly.

Penelope felt a small thrill of excitement. She was lost—truly lost, in a place no one else seemed to ever go. But instead of fear, a wave of exhilaration washed over her. This was exactly what she had always wanted—a chance to explore something completely unknown.

As she continued walking, something caught her eye. Just ahead, through a small break in the trees, she saw a faint glow. It was soft and warm, like the last light of a sunset, but it was coming from the ground. Penelope hesitated for a moment, then moved toward the light.

She pushed aside a curtain of vines and stepped into a small clearing. At the center of the clearing was an enormous tree—larger than any she had seen before. Its trunk was thick and gnarled, its bark covered in strange, twisting patterns that seemed to glow faintly in the dim light. But it wasn't the tree that had caught Penelope's attention. It was the roots. They spread out from the base of the tree like fingers, and between them, nestled in the moss and leaves, was a small, glowing object.

Penelope knelt down, her breath catching in her throat. The object was smooth and round, no bigger than an apple, and it pulsed gently with a soft, golden light. It looked like a stone, but it was unlike any stone Penelope had ever seen.

She reached out to touch it, her fingers trembling slightly. The moment her hand brushed against the stone, a strange warmth spread through her body. It wasn't unpleasant—just...odd. It was as if the stone recognized her, as if it had been waiting for her all this time.

Penelope picked up the stone, cradling it in her hands. The light seemed to brighten for a moment, and then something even stranger happened. The tree—silent and still just moments before—began to whisper.

At first, Penelope thought it was the wind. But then she realized the sound was coming from the tree itself, from deep within its branches and roots. The whisper was soft, almost musical, like a distant voice carried on the breeze.

Penelope's heart raced. She leaned in closer, trying to catch the words. But the whisper was too faint, too elusive.

Suddenly, the glow from the stone flickered, and the whispering stopped. The forest fell silent once again, leaving Penelope standing alone in the clearing, holding the strange, glowing stone.

She looked down at the stone in her hands, her mind racing with questions. What was this place? Why had the stone called to her? And what was the tree trying to tell her?

One thing was certain: this forest was not ordinary. It was a place of secrets, of mysteries hidden just beneath the surface. And Penelope Pine, with her boundless curiosity, had just scratched the surface of something far greater than she had ever imagined.

With a determined look in her eyes, Penelope tucked the stone into her pocket. Whatever this forest was, it was hers to explore. And no matter what dangers or wonders lay ahead, she was ready to uncover every single one of them.

She turned and began walking deeper into the forest, the faint glow of the stone lighting her way.

Chapter 2: The Whispering Tree

Penelope had always believed there was more to the world than what met the eye. After discovering the strange glowing stone and hearing the faint whisper from the ancient tree, she was certain of it. The forest was no ordinary place, and neither was her adventure. What she didn't know yet was just how vast and mysterious it truly was.

The glowing stone felt warm in her pocket as she continued through the thickening woods. Every now and then, she glanced around, half-expecting to see more strange things—talking animals or hidden doorways—but nothing came. It was just her, the trees, and the ever-present soft hum in the air.

After what felt like hours of walking, Penelope noticed something unusual in the distance. Through the tall, towering trees, she could see a giant shape that seemed to rise high above the rest of the forest. Its bark was darker than the other trees, its branches spreading like a canopy over the forest floor. There was something majestic, almost ancient, about the way it loomed in the distance, as though it had stood there for centuries, watching over the land.

Penelope felt a pull toward it. She didn't understand why, but every step she took seemed to bring her closer to it, as though the tree itself were calling her. The closer she got, the more she noticed strange details. The other trees bent slightly in its direction, their leaves rustling softly, as if in reverence.

At last, she stepped into another clearing, and there it was.

The tree was enormous, its thick roots curling out of the ground like massive, knotted ropes. Its trunk was so wide that Penelope couldn't even imagine how long it must have taken to grow so large. Its bark was dark and etched with symbols—spirals, lines, and patterns that reminded Penelope of old stories she had read about forgotten civilizations. High above her head, the branches spread in all directions, their leaves shimmering faintly in the sunlight.

Penelope's breath caught in her throat as she gazed up at the tree. There was something alive about it, something that felt far older than the forest itself. And then she heard it again—the whisper.

It was faint at first, a soft murmur carried on the wind. But as she took a step closer, the sound grew clearer. It wasn't the wind. It was the tree.

Penelope froze, her heart pounding. Could a tree really whisper?

She took another step forward, her hands trembling. The whisper grew louder, still soft but now unmistakable. It was like a voice, though the words were unclear, blending together in a melodic hum. She strained to listen, trying to catch the meaning behind the sound. It was as if the tree was speaking directly to her, telling her something important.

Her eyes widened as she realized the voice wasn't just random. It was trying to tell her something—something about the forest.

Cautiously, she placed her hand on the rough bark of the tree. The moment her fingers made contact, the whispering stopped.

For a moment, there was nothing but silence. Penelope frowned and took a step back, confused. But just as she was about to give up, the stone in her pocket began to glow again, casting a warm light around her.

And then, the whisper returned. But this time, it wasn't just a hum. It was words.

"Welcome, seeker of secrets."

Penelope gasped, her eyes wide as she looked around. The voice was soft, almost like an old, wise person speaking from a great distance, but it was clear. The tree was speaking to her.

"H-hello?" she whispered, feeling a little foolish for talking to a tree. But in this strange forest, nothing seemed impossible anymore.

The tree's branches swayed slightly, as if in response. "You are the first to hear me in many ages, young one. The forest has waited long for one such as you."

Penelope's heart raced. "Who...who are you?"

"I am the Heart of the Forest, the keeper of its secrets," the tree replied, its voice gentle but full of power. "For centuries, I have watched over this land, guiding those who seek knowledge and wonder. Few have come in search of its magic, and fewer still have been worthy to hear the whispers of the forest."

Penelope's mind swirled with questions. "Why...why me?" she asked. "I'm just...me."

The tree's branches rustled, as though amused. "Because, Penelope Pine, you possess the gift of curiosity, a gift more powerful than you know. This forest responds to curiosity, to those who seek answers beyond the ordinary. It called you here because you were willing to listen."

Penelope blinked in surprise. "You...you know my name?"

"I know all who enter this place," the tree said. "But you are different from the others. You see, this forest is not merely a collection of trees and plants. It is a living, breathing entity, filled with magic, mystery, and wonder. And it has chosen you."

Penelope's mouth went dry. "Chosen me? For what?"

"To explore its hidden places, to uncover its forgotten secrets," the tree replied. "There are many places within this forest, each more wondrous than the last. Some are beautiful, some are dangerous, but all are magical. And I will guide you, if you are brave enough to follow the whispers."

Penelope felt a thrill of excitement rush through her. This was exactly what she had always dreamed of—a true adventure, filled with mysteries waiting to be solved.

"What do I need to do?" she asked, her voice trembling slightly with anticipation.

"Listen to the land," the tree whispered. "Follow the whispers of the wind, the rustle of the leaves, the glow of the stone you carry. They will guide you to places where magic still lingers."

Penelope reached into her pocket and pulled out the glowing stone. It pulsed gently in her hand, as though responding to the tree's words.

"There is a place not far from here," the tree continued. "A garden, long forgotten, where the flowers bloom only under the light of the moon. It is said that the spirits of the forest gather there, though no one has seen them in many years. Go there, Penelope. Find the garden, and you will uncover the first of many secrets."

Penelope's heart raced. "How will I find it?"

The tree's branches rustled again, and suddenly, one of the glowing symbols on its trunk shifted. It moved like a shadow, sliding across the bark to form a new shape—a path, winding through the forest. It was a map, etched into the tree's surface.

Penelope stepped closer, studying the intricate lines and curves. The map showed her where to go, leading her deeper into the woods, to a place she had never seen before.

"Follow the path," the tree whispered. "But be wary, for not all who wander the forest have pure intentions. There are those who seek to control its magic, to use it for selfish gain. You must trust your instincts, and let your curiosity guide you."

Penelope nodded, feeling a mixture of excitement and nervousness. She had always wanted an adventure, and now, it was right in front of her. The forest was filled with secrets, just waiting to be uncovered, and she was the one chosen to explore them.

"I won't let you down," she said, her voice firm.

"I know you won't," the tree whispered, its voice growing softer. "Go now, Penelope Pine. The forest is waiting."

With that, the glowing symbols on the tree began to fade, and the whispering grew fainter, until it was gone completely. Penelope stood there for a moment, staring up at the massive tree, feeling a strange sense of awe and purpose.

Then, with the glowing stone in her hand and the map etched in her memory, she turned and began walking deeper into the forest, toward the forgotten garden.

The adventure had truly begun.

Chapter 3: The Enchanted Map

Penelope couldn't stop thinking about the Whispering Tree. Even as she ventured farther into the forest, toward the forgotten garden it had told her about, her mind was racing with questions. Why had the forest chosen her? What secrets did it hide? And who were the others—those with impure intentions—who sought to control its magic?

The forest felt alive around her, as though it were watching her every move. The air was thick with the scent of moss and earth, and the light filtering through the canopy above seemed to glow a little brighter than before. Penelope had always felt a connection to nature, but this was different. She was no longer just an observer; she was part of something much bigger.

As she walked, the stone in her pocket pulsed gently, guiding her. She didn't know how, but she trusted it completely. It was as though the stone and the forest were connected, and they both wanted her to succeed.

After what felt like hours, Penelope came upon a small clearing. In the center stood another massive tree, though not as large as the Whispering Tree. This one had a twisted trunk and branches that stretched toward the sky like long, bony fingers. There was something different about this tree—it wasn't just a part of the forest. It felt…important.

Penelope hesitated for a moment, her eyes scanning the tree. The symbols on its bark were faint, but they were there, just like on the Whispering Tree. She had a strange feeling that this tree, too, had something to reveal.

Slowly, she approached it. As she got closer, she noticed something peculiar—a small opening at the base of the tree, just big enough for her hand to fit inside. Without thinking, she reached into the hollow, her fingers brushing against something cool and smooth.

She pulled it out slowly, her heart racing. In her hand was an old, rolled-up parchment. It was tied with a thin strip of leather, its edges worn with age. The moment it was free from the tree, the parchment began to glow softly, much like the stone in her pocket.

Penelope's breath caught in her throat. She carefully untied the leather strap and unrolled the parchment. What she saw took her breath away.

It was a map—a glowing, enchanted map of the entire forest.

The lines on the parchment shimmered with light, shifting and moving as though they were alive. Penelope's eyes widened as she realized the map showed not just the trees and paths, but places—hidden places—marked with symbols and strange drawings. There were small illustrations of mysterious objects, glowing creatures, and what appeared to be hidden doorways scattered across the map.

The most incredible part, however, was that as Penelope looked at it, the map seemed to respond to her thoughts. When she focused on a particular part of the forest, the details in that area sharpened, the symbols growing clearer. It was as if the map was attuned to her, revealing exactly what she needed to see.

Her heart raced with excitement. The tree had not only guided her to the garden, but it had given her a tool to explore the entire forest—a map that showed places of magic, danger, and wonder. But there was more.

As she continued to examine the map, a new symbol appeared, glowing brighter than the rest. It was a small, intricate mark—a spiral surrounded by what looked like leaves. The moment Penelope saw it, she felt a tug deep inside her, as if the forest itself was telling her that this place was important.

The symbol was located in a part of the forest she had never seen before, far beyond the boundaries of Windy Hollow. It was deep within the forest, in an area that seemed untouched by time or people. Beneath the symbol, in small, glowing letters, was a single word: Sanctuary.

Penelope's curiosity flared to life. What was this place? And why had the map revealed it to her?

She knew one thing for sure: she had to find it.

But first, she needed to figure out how to read the map properly. It was unlike any map she'd ever seen, not just because of its magical glow, but because it wasn't static. The lines and symbols shifted as she looked at them, revealing new details or changing completely depending on her focus. It felt alive, as if it were trying to show her the way.

Penelope sat down at the base of the tree, the map spread out before her. She closed her eyes for a moment, trying to calm the excitement bubbling up inside her. She had always loved maps—there was something thrilling about looking at the unknown and knowing that somewhere, hidden among those lines, was an adventure waiting to be discovered. But this map was different. This map wasn't just about showing her where to go; it was guiding her.

She opened her eyes and focused on the glowing word: Sanctuary. As she did, the map shifted again, zooming in on the area around the symbol. The details grew clearer. Penelope saw a path winding through the trees, leading to what looked like an ancient stone archway. Beyond that, the map faded into swirling lines and symbols, as though even the magic of the map couldn't fully reveal what lay beyond.

Penelope's pulse quickened. An ancient sanctuary hidden deep within the forest? It sounded exactly like the kind of place the Whispering Tree had wanted her to find.

She rolled up the map carefully, tucking it into her satchel along with the glowing stone. The forest had given her a tool—no, a gift—and she was going to use it. There were so many places marked on the map, so many mysteries to uncover, but her instincts told her to follow the Sanctuary first.

As she stood up, a rustling sound caught her attention. For a moment, she thought it might be the wind, but then she heard it again—closer this time. It wasn't the sound of leaves or branches. It was something else. Something moving.

Penelope's heart raced as she turned, scanning the clearing. At first, she saw nothing. The trees stood tall and still, their shadows stretching across the ground. But then, out of the corner of her eye, she saw it—a figure, darting between the trees at the edge of the clearing.

Her breath caught in her throat. She wasn't alone.

The figure was small, quick, and hard to make out. It moved like a shadow, disappearing behind one tree only to reappear behind another. Penelope squinted, trying to get a better look, but the figure stayed just out of reach, as if it didn't want to be seen.

"Hello?" Penelope called, her voice trembling slightly.

There was no answer. The figure paused for a moment, then darted away, disappearing into the forest. Penelope stood frozen, her heart pounding in her chest. Who—or what—was that? It didn't feel like a threat, but it was clear that someone—or something—was watching her.

She glanced back at the tree, her mind racing. The Whispering Tree had warned her that there were others in the forest, people with impure intentions. Could that figure have been one of them? Or was it something else entirely? She didn't know, but she had a feeling she would find out soon enough.

Penelope took a deep breath, steeling herself. Whatever was out there, she couldn't let it scare her away. The forest was vast, and it was filled with wonders and dangers alike, but she had been chosen for this adventure. She wasn't going to back down now.

With one last glance at the twisted tree, Penelope set off in the direction the map had shown her. The path to the Sanctuary awaited, and with it, the next chapter of her adventure.

As she walked, the glowing stone in her pocket pulsed again, a steady rhythm that matched the beating of her heart. The map had marked the way, but Penelope knew that the journey ahead would not be easy. The forest was alive, and it had many secrets yet to reveal.

But Penelope Pine was ready. She had the map, the stone, and the forest's whispers to guide her. And no matter what challenges lay ahead, she knew she was exactly where she was meant to be.

The adventure was only just beginning.

Chapter 4: The Talking Squirrel

Penelope trekked deeper into the forest, the glowing stone in her pocket softly pulsing as she clutched the enchanted map. The air was cooler here, the canopy overhead thick with leaves, filtering the sunlight into gentle, green hues. It had been hours since the strange figure darted away, and Penelope's nerves had settled, though she remained on edge. She knew she wasn't alone, but for now, the forest felt quiet, as if it were watching, waiting for her to take the next step.

The map had marked her path toward the Sanctuary, and as Penelope walked, she couldn't help but notice how the forest seemed to change around her. The trees here were older, their trunks wider and more twisted, their branches heavy with thick vines. Strange flowers bloomed along the edges of the path, their petals glowing faintly in the dim light. The deeper Penelope went, the more she felt as though she were entering a world entirely separate from the one she had always known.

She stopped for a moment to catch her breath and pulled the map out of her satchel. The glowing lines had shifted slightly, showing her that she was getting closer to her destination. But something new caught her eye—an intricate drawing near the edge of the map, not far from her current location. It wasn't marked with a symbol of danger, like some of the other areas on the map, but there was something about the way the lines swirled and looped around the drawing that intrigued her.

"What is that?" Penelope muttered to herself.

Before she could study it any further, a sudden rustling sound in the bushes behind her made her jump. She spun around, her heart racing, expecting to see another shadowy figure, or perhaps even one of the magical creatures hinted at in the map. But there was nothing—just the wind gently stirring the leaves.

Penelope let out a nervous laugh. "Come on, Penelope. You're jumping at shadows," she muttered.

She turned back to the map, but before she could focus on it again, a small, insistent voice broke the silence.

"Well, well, well. What have we here? A human, wandering alone in the depths of the Whispering Woods?"

Penelope froze. She slowly lowered the map and glanced around, searching for the source of the voice. "Who's there?" she asked, her voice trembling slightly.

The bushes rustled again, and a small figure darted out from behind the nearest tree, stopping directly in front of her. Penelope blinked in surprise.

It was a squirrel—a perfectly ordinary-looking squirrel, with bushy fur, bright eyes, and a twitching nose. But what wasn't ordinary, of course, was that this squirrel had just spoken.

Penelope stared at the creature, her mind racing. Had she really just heard that? She must have—there was no one else around.

"Don't look so shocked," the squirrel said, sitting back on its haunches and folding its tiny arms across its chest. "It's terribly rude to stare, you know."

"I—uh—I'm sorry," Penelope stammered. "I've just never met a talking squirrel before."

The squirrel tilted its head to the side, regarding her with a mixture of curiosity and amusement. "Well, now you have. Consider yourself lucky. Not everyone in the forest is as friendly as I am."

Penelope finally found her voice. "What...what's your name?"

The squirrel puffed out its chest, clearly pleased by the question. "I am Jasper," he said grandly. "And you, human, are quite fortunate to have crossed paths with me. Few travellers are so lucky as to have the guidance of one such as myself."

Penelope couldn't help but smile. "Well, it's nice to meet you, Jasper. My name is Penelope."

Jasper twitched his nose. "Penelope, eh? Not a bad name. A bit long for my taste, but it'll do." He hopped closer, his bright eyes narrowing slightly as he looked her up and down. "So, Penelope, what brings a young human like you all the way out here? Don't you know the Whispering Woods are no place for wandering?"

"I'm not wandering," Penelope said, holding up the glowing map. "I'm following this."

Jasper's eyes widened at the sight of the map, and he leapt up onto a nearby tree stump, peering at it intently. "An enchanted map? And not just any enchanted map, by the looks of it. That's old magic, that is." He looked up at her, a hint of respect in his eyes. "Where did you get it?"

Penelope explained how she had found the map inside the tree after her encounter with the Whispering Tree. As she spoke, Jasper listened intently, his tail twitching occasionally, though he said nothing until she finished.

"Well, well," he said thoughtfully. "Seems the forest has taken a liking to you. That map will lead you to all sorts of places, though I imagine not all of them are friendly."

Penelope nodded, feeling the weight of the responsibility settling on her shoulders. "I'm trying to find a place called the Sanctuary," she said, pointing to the symbol on the map.

Jasper's eyes narrowed, and he let out a low whistle. "The Sanctuary, huh? Now that's a place of legend. Few have ever seen it, and those who have...well, let's just say they don't come back the same."

Penelope's curiosity flared. "What do you mean?"

Jasper twitched his nose again and hopped down from the stump. "The Sanctuary is old, older than the forest itself, some say. It's a place of great magic, where the lines between this world and the next blur. Some go seeking wisdom, others power. But whatever you seek, the Sanctuary will test you. It only reveals its true self to those who are worthy."

Penelope felt a shiver run down her spine. "And how do I know if I'm worthy?"

Jasper shrugged. "That's for the Sanctuary to decide. But don't worry, you've got me now. I'll guide you there safely—well, as safely as one can manage in these parts."

Penelope smiled, feeling a surge of relief. "Thank you, Jasper. I could really use a guide."

Jasper waved a tiny paw dismissively. "Oh, it's no trouble. Besides, I haven't had a decent adventure in ages." He hopped up onto her shoulder, his tail flicking against her cheek. "Now, let's get going. The Sanctuary isn't going to find itself."

Penelope couldn't help but laugh. With Jasper by her side—or rather, on her shoulder—she felt a little more confident about the journey ahead. The talking squirrel was full of charm, and despite his small size, he seemed to know a great deal about the forest and its secrets.

As they walked, Jasper chattered away, telling her all sorts of things about the forest. He pointed out different plants and trees, some of which had magical properties, and warned her of dangerous creatures that lurked in the shadows. Penelope listened intently, absorbing every bit of information. She had always been curious about the world around her, and now that curiosity was being rewarded in ways she had never imagined.

"So, how does a squirrel come to know so much about magic?" Penelope asked as they walked.

Jasper puffed up his chest again. "Ah, well, I wasn't always a mere squirrel, you know. Long ago, I was a creature of great importance—a guardian of the forest, tasked with protecting its secrets. But, alas, things don't always go as planned. There was…an incident, shall we say, and now I'm a squirrel. But that doesn't mean I've lost my knowledge."

Penelope raised an eyebrow. "An incident?"

Jasper twitched his tail. "Yes, yes. It's a long story. Perhaps I'll tell you one day. For now, let's focus on getting to the Sanctuary, shall we?"

They continued on, following the path the map had shown. The forest around them grew quieter as they went, the sounds of birds and insects fading into the background. The air felt thicker here, almost as if the trees were watching their every move.

Penelope kept her hand on the glowing stone in her pocket, feeling its steady pulse as they walked. The map was leading her to the Sanctuary, but she couldn't shake the feeling that something—or someone—was following them.

Jasper seemed to sense her unease. "Don't worry, Penelope," he said from her shoulder. "Whatever's out there, it won't catch us off guard. I've got sharp eyes, and you've got that map. We'll be fine."

Penelope nodded, though she still felt a flicker of uncertainty. She wasn't afraid, exactly, but the forest was full of unknowns, and she knew that anything could happen.

As they pressed on, the trees around them grew even thicker, their branches weaving together overhead to form a dark, tangled canopy. The path narrowed, and the air grew colder. Penelope's breath formed small clouds in the air, and Jasper's fur bristled against her cheek.

"We're close," Jasper said quietly. "I can feel it."

Penelope glanced down at the map, her heart pounding. The symbol for the Sanctuary was glowing brightly now, pulsing in time with the stone in her pocket. They were almost there.

She took a deep breath and stepped forward, feeling the weight of the forest's magic all around her. The Sanctuary awaited.

Chapter 5: The Forgotten Garden

The deeper Penelope and Jasper ventured into the forest, the stranger and more magical the surroundings became. The trees around them grew thicker, their branches twisting into intricate patterns overhead, blocking out most of the sunlight. A faint glow still emanated from the enchanted map, guiding them toward their next destination.

Penelope's curiosity was on fire. She had followed the path marked on the map, leading her and Jasper toward a place that intrigued her deeply—the Forgotten Garden. It was marked with delicate drawings of plants and symbols that shimmered on the map, and she couldn't help but wonder what awaited them.

"Do you know anything about this garden, Jasper?" Penelope asked as they walked. The squirrel perched on her shoulder, his tiny paws resting on her hair as he peered ahead.

Jasper scratched his chin thoughtfully. "The Forgotten Garden, you say? Hmm, I've heard whispers of it over the years. Long ago, it was said to be a place of beauty, filled with magical plants that bloomed under the moonlight. The forest spirits would gather there to tell their stories, but that was ages ago. No one's been there in quite some time."

"Why not?" Penelope asked, looking at the path ahead, her excitement tempered by curiosity.

"Well, it's been hidden," Jasper replied. "The garden was abandoned after the last of the forest spirits disappeared. Most don't even remember it exists anymore. But if your map is leading us there, it must mean the magic is still alive. Or at least, something is."

Penelope felt a twinge of anticipation. A forgotten garden where the plants came to life at night? It sounded like something out of a dream.

The forest around them grew quieter, the usual sounds of birds and rustling leaves fading into the background. Even the air felt different—cooler, heavier, as though they were stepping into a place untouched by time.

Finally, they came upon a high wall of tangled vines, overgrown and thick with brambles. Penelope stopped, glancing at the map to confirm that they had arrived. The glowing lines showed the entrance just ahead, though the wall of vines appeared impenetrable at first glance.

"This is it," she whispered, her eyes scanning the overgrowth. "But how do we get inside?"

Jasper leapt off her shoulder and scurried toward the vines, his sharp claws digging into the bark of a nearby tree. "Give me a moment. There's usually a trick to these sorts of things," he said as he climbed swiftly, inspecting the wall.

Penelope knelt down, studying the vines more closely. She reached out, brushing her fingers against the thick green tendrils. The moment she touched them, the vines seemed to shiver, a soft rustling sound filling the air. Before her eyes, the vines began to pull away from one another, slowly unwinding like a knot being loosened.

Penelope gasped as the vines revealed a hidden stone archway, its surface covered in ancient symbols similar to those on the map. Beyond the archway, a faint light flickered, as though something inside the garden was calling them forward.

"Well done!" Jasper called from the tree, his eyes twinkling. "Looks like the garden recognizes you."

Penelope smiled, feeling a thrill of excitement. She stepped through the archway, her heart pounding with anticipation. Jasper quickly scampered down the tree and joined her, darting past her legs to investigate.

The Forgotten Garden was unlike anything Penelope had ever seen. As soon as they crossed the threshold, the air became warmer, filled with the sweet scent of flowers and rich, earthy soil. The garden was vast, stretching out before them in all directions, though much of it was overgrown with wild plants and creeping vines. Stone paths wound through the foliage, and in the center of the garden stood an ancient fountain, its once-glorious structure now cracked and covered in moss.

But even in its forgotten state, the garden was beautiful. Flowers of every shape and color grew in abundance, their petals glistening as if covered in dew. Giant ferns swayed gently in the breeze, and the trees overhead sparkled with tiny lights, like fireflies caught in their branches.

"This place is incredible," Penelope whispered, turning in a slow circle to take it all in. "How could anyone forget something like this?"

Jasper perched on the edge of the fountain, his nose twitching as he looked around. "The forest hides what it wants to hide. It chooses who sees its secrets."

Penelope wandered deeper into the garden, her eyes drawn to the plants that seemed to pulse with faint light. The map had hinted that this garden was more than just a collection of magical plants, and Penelope could feel it in the air. There was something alive here, something waiting to be discovered.

As the sun dipped below the horizon, the garden began to change. The colors of the plants grew more vibrant, and the soft glow that had been barely noticeable in the daylight became more pronounced. It was as though the garden was waking up, coming to life as the night settled over the forest.

Penelope watched in awe as the flowers around her began to move. Their petals unfurled, and the plants themselves started to sway, as if responding to an invisible rhythm. The vines that had seemed dormant during the day now twined through the air, creating delicate patterns above their heads. The entire garden was in motion, alive with magic.

And then, Penelope heard it—the sound of voices. At first, she thought it was the wind, but as she listened more closely, she realized the voices were soft, melodic, and full of wisdom. They seemed to come from the plants themselves, as though the garden was whispering its secrets.

Jasper's eyes widened as he hopped onto Penelope's shoulder again. "They're speaking! Do you hear them?"

Penelope nodded, her heart racing. "What are they saying?"

The voices were too faint to make out at first, but as Penelope focused, the words became clearer. The plants were telling stories—stories of the past, of the garden's creation, and of the beings who once tended it. Each plant seemed to have its own tale, weaving together the history of the garden and the forest itself.

Penelope walked slowly through the garden, listening to the voices. The trees spoke of ancient forest spirits who had danced under the stars, tending the plants and filling the air with music. The flowers told tales of long-lost visitors who had come seeking wisdom, only to leave with their hearts full of wonder. Even the stones beneath her feet seemed to hum with the memories of those who had walked the paths before her.

"This place..." Penelope whispered, "it's like it remembers everything."

Jasper nodded. "The garden has been waiting for someone like you, Penelope. It remembers, but it's also alive. The magic here is still strong, even after all this time."

As Penelope walked, she noticed that the plants seemed to respond to her presence. The flowers leaned toward her, their soft petals brushing against her hands as she passed. The vines twisted and curled, creating archways above her head. It was as though the garden recognized her, welcoming her as its first visitor in ages.

But there was more. As the garden came to life around her, Penelope realized that the voices were not just telling stories—they were offering guidance.

One voice in particular stood out, stronger than the rest. It came from a tall, glowing plant near the fountain, its leaves shimmering with light. Penelope approached it, drawn to its soft, melodic tone.

The plant's voice was clear and gentle. "Child of curiosity, you have found the Forgotten Garden. Here, the stories of the past are woven into the magic of the earth. But you seek more, do you not?"

Penelope's heart skipped a beat. "Yes," she whispered. "I'm searching for a place called the Sanctuary."

The plant's leaves rustled softly. "The Sanctuary lies beyond the garden, hidden deep within the heart of the forest. But to find it, you must listen to the whispers of the land. Follow the path that the moonlight reveals."

Penelope looked up at the sky, where the first sliver of the moon had appeared. Its light cast long shadows across the garden, illuminating the stone paths and the glowing plants.

Jasper hopped down from her shoulder and sniffed the air. "Looks like we've got our next clue. Moonlight paths, huh? Sounds mysterious."

Penelope smiled, feeling a surge of determination. The Forgotten Garden had given her more than just stories—it had given her direction. The Sanctuary was close, and now she knew how to find it.

"Thank you," Penelope said, bowing her head to the glowing plant. "I'll follow the path."

The plant's light flickered softly, as though acknowledging her. "The forest has many secrets, child. Tread carefully, and trust in the magic that guides you."

With that, the garden's voices grew softer, blending into the night. The plants continued to dance in the moonlight, their soft glow lighting the way forward.

Penelope took a deep breath and turned to Jasper. "Are you ready?"

Jasper grinned. "Always."

Together, they followed the moonlit path that stretched out before them, deeper into the forest, toward the next part of their adventure.

Chapter 6: The Moonlit Lake

The forest seemed quieter as Penelope and Jasper continued their journey along the moonlit path. The glowing map in Penelope's hand pulsed gently, revealing their next destination. Every step felt like a deeper dive into the mysteries of the forest, each discovery leading her closer to the elusive Sanctuary. As they left the Forgotten Garden behind, the moon shone brightly overhead, casting long shadows on the forest floor.

Jasper scampered ahead, his tiny paws barely making a sound as he moved through the underbrush. "According to that map of yours," he called back to Penelope, "we're heading toward a lake, right? I've heard rumours about a magical lake hidden deep in the forest, but I always thought it was just a story."

Penelope looked down at the map. The lake was marked by a crescent moon symbol, with shimmering waves drawn around it. She traced the lines with her finger and nodded. "Yes, it's called the Moonlit Lake. The map shows that it only appears under the full moon."

Jasper's eyes widened. "A lake that only exists during the full moon? Now that's something you don't see every day. I wonder what's hiding in those waters."

Penelope smiled. "Let's find out."

They pressed on, following the trail as it wound through the thick forest. The trees around them grew taller and closer together, their branches reaching out like arms overhead, creating a canopy that blocked out most of the moonlight. Only small slivers of silvery light filtered through, giving the path a dreamlike quality.

As they walked, the air grew cooler, and Penelope could hear the faint sound of water in the distance. It was a soft, rhythmic sound, like the gentle lapping of waves against a shore. Her pulse quickened as they drew closer. The Moonlit Lake was near.

Finally, they emerged from the dense trees into an open clearing. Penelope gasped in awe. There, in the center of the clearing, lay a shimmering lake, its surface glowing softly under the light of the full moon. The water was so still, it looked like a mirror reflecting the sky above, the stars twinkling in its depths.

"This is incredible," Penelope whispered, stepping forward.

Jasper hopped onto a nearby rock, his eyes wide with wonder. "Well, I'll be! It really does exist!"

The lake was surrounded by smooth stones, their surfaces worn smooth by time and weather. Tall reeds swayed gently along the shore, their tips glowing faintly in the moonlight. Everything about the lake felt magical, as if it had been untouched for centuries, waiting for the right moment to reveal itself.

Penelope knelt by the water's edge and peered into the depths. The water was crystal clear, and she could see down to the lakebed, which was scattered with smooth pebbles and strange, shimmering objects. Her heart raced as she realized what she was seeing—beneath the surface, hidden among the rocks and reeds, were ancient treasures.

"There's something down there," she whispered.

Jasper's ears perked up. "Treasures, you say?" He scurried down to the water's edge, his nose twitching with excitement. "I knew it! This lake is full of secrets."

Penelope's fingers brushed the surface of the water. It was cool to the touch, but not cold. The moment her hand made contact, small ripples spread across the lake, disturbing its glass-like stillness. The ripples glowed softly in the moonlight, and Penelope watched in awe as the light seemed to react to her touch.

Suddenly, the water in front of her began to shift. Slowly, a series of glowing symbols appeared on the lake's surface, forming a delicate, swirling pattern. Penelope recognized them instantly—they were the same symbols that had been etched into the Whispering Tree and the map.

"It's magic," she whispered, her heart pounding. "The lake is enchanted."

Jasper leaned over her shoulder, his eyes wide. "What do you think it means?"

Penelope stared at the glowing symbols, trying to decipher their meaning. They seemed to be pointing toward something, their light growing brighter the deeper she looked into the water. And then she saw it—at the very bottom of the lake, half-buried in the silt and sand, was an object that glowed with a faint, golden light.

Without thinking, Penelope slipped off her shoes and waded into the water. It was cool against her skin, but not unpleasant. She moved carefully, her eyes fixed on the glowing object below. As she waded deeper, the water reached her knees, then her waist, but it remained calm, as though it were welcoming her.

Jasper paced nervously on the shore, his tail flicking back and forth. "Are you sure about this, Penelope? I mean, magical lakes and ancient treasures sound great and all, but I don't like the idea of you diving into mysterious waters. Who knows what's down there?"

Penelope smiled reassuringly. "I'll be fine, Jasper. I have a feeling the lake wants me to find this."

With that, she took a deep breath and dove beneath the surface. The water was clear and surprisingly warm as she swam down toward the glowing object. The deeper she went, the brighter the light became, until she could see the object clearly.

It was a small chest, made of stone and covered in intricate carvings that glowed faintly in the moonlight. The chest looked ancient, as though it had been resting at the bottom of the lake for centuries, waiting for someone to find it.

Penelope reached out and gently touched the chest. The moment her fingers brushed the stone, the carvings flared to life, glowing brightly. The chest seemed to recognize her touch, and with a soft click, the lid opened.

Inside the chest, resting on a bed of smooth, black stones, was a single key. The key was made of shimmering silver, and its handle was shaped like a crescent moon. It glowed softly in the water, as though imbued with the magic of the lake itself.

Penelope's breath caught in her throat. This was no ordinary key—she could feel the magic radiating from it. This key was important, and she knew without a doubt that it was part of her quest.

She carefully took the key from the chest and tucked it into the pocket of her satchel. The moment she did, the glowing symbols on the lake's surface began to fade, and the water returned to its still, mirror-like state.

Penelope swam back to the surface, gasping for air as she broke through the water. Jasper was waiting anxiously on the shore, his eyes wide with concern.

"Penelope! Are you okay? What did you find?"

Penelope waded back to the shore, her heart racing with excitement. She climbed out of the water and held up the silver key, its soft glow reflecting the moonlight.

Jasper's eyes widened. "A key? What does it open?"

"I don't know yet," Penelope admitted, her fingers tracing the delicate curves of the crescent-shaped handle. "But it has to be important. The lake wouldn't have hidden it otherwise."

Jasper nodded, his excitement growing. "So, we've got a magical key from a moonlit lake. That's got to lead to something big."

Penelope smiled, feeling a surge of anticipation. The lake had been full of magic, and she knew this key was the next step in uncovering the forest's secrets.

As they stood by the lake, the full moon shining brightly above them, Penelope felt a sense of purpose settle over her. The enchanted map had led her to the Moonlit Lake, and now it would guide her to the next destination—wherever that might be.

But one thing was certain: the key she now carried was important. It felt like the forest was giving her the tools she needed to find the Sanctuary, one step at a time.

"We should get moving," Penelope said, tucking the key safely into her satchel. "The moon won't be out forever, and there's still so much to discover."

Jasper nodded. "Agreed. Onward we go!"

With the moonlit path guiding them once more, Penelope and Jasper set off into the forest, the silver key glinting softly in her bag. The Moonlit Lake had revealed its treasure, but the adventure was far from over.

As they disappeared into the trees, the lake behind them shimmered one last time before vanishing into the darkness, hidden once again until the next full moon.

Chapter 7: The Invisible Bridge

The next destination on the enchanted map was unlike anything Penelope had encountered so far. After leaving the Moonlit Lake behind, she and Jasper had followed the glowing path through the forest for hours, the key from the lake tucked safely in Penelope's satchel. The map's shimmering lines had shifted again, guiding them toward an island, though no lake or river appeared on the map itself. Instead, a delicate, intricate drawing of a bridge lay in the middle of a wide, blank space, surrounded by strange symbols that Penelope couldn't quite decipher.

"We're heading for an island," Penelope said aloud, turning the map over in her hands. "But there's no water, no river, or anything. How can there be an island with no way to reach it?"

Jasper, perched on her shoulder, twitched his nose thoughtfully. "If the map says there's an island, then there's an island. But I've never heard of one in these parts. And if the forest wants to hide something, it hides it well."

Penelope nodded. The map had already led them to places she'd never imagined—forgotten gardens, moonlit lakes—so an invisible island didn't seem too far-fetched. But there was something about the island's location that made her uneasy. It wasn't just hidden; it seemed unreachable.

The two of them pressed on, the trees growing sparser as they moved deeper into the forest. Soon, the thick woods gave way to a wide, open expanse. Penelope stopped at the edge of a large clearing. It stretched out as far as she could see, a flat, barren plain of dry grass and scattered stones, with no sign of a lake, a river, or even an island. The enchanted map pulsed in her hand, indicating that the island lay straight ahead, but there was nothing in front of her except endless, empty space.

"This doesn't make sense," Penelope muttered, staring at the map. "We're right where it says we should be, but there's no bridge. No island."

Jasper hopped down from her shoulder and padded toward the edge of the clearing. He squinted, his nose twitching as he surveyed the landscape. "Hmm, I don't see anything either. But if there's a bridge here, it's not one we can see. Maybe it's hidden."

Penelope looked out over the empty expanse again. Hidden. She had seen enough magic in the forest by now to know that things weren't always as they seemed. There was a bridge here, the map said so—but how could they cross something that wasn't visible?

Jasper scurried over to the edge of the clearing and tapped his foot against the ground. "Nothing here but rocks and grass. No sign of a river or a lake anywhere."

Penelope stepped forward, scanning the horizon. "It has to be here. The map says it is." She thought for a moment, remembering the strange symbols drawn around the bridge on the map. They seemed to shimmer in her mind, almost like a riddle waiting to be solved. She closed her eyes, focusing on the feeling the forest had given her since the very beginning—the sense that anything was possible here, that magic lived in the spaces between reality and imagination.

"Maybe we can't see it," Penelope said softly, opening her eyes. "Maybe the bridge is only visible if we believe in it."

Jasper glanced up at her, one eyebrow raised. "Believe in it? That's a bit far-fetched, don't you think?"

Penelope shook her head. "Not in this forest. Think about it—everything here is built on magic, on things that shouldn't be possible. If we only see what we expect to see, then maybe we won't see the bridge because we don't believe it's there."

Jasper scratched his chin, then shrugged. "Well, stranger things have happened." He hopped back onto her shoulder. "So, we just...believe there's a bridge, and then it shows up? I suppose it's worth a try."

Penelope took a deep breath and stared out over the empty space in front of them. It seemed impossible—how could a bridge appear just because she wanted it to? But the forest had already taught her that nothing was truly impossible, not here.

She closed her eyes again, this time with a clear intention in her mind. She pictured the bridge in her mind—an invisible structure stretching out across the clearing, connecting the forest to an island that lay hidden beyond. She imagined the air around her shifting, the impossible becoming real, until the bridge appeared before her, solid and steady.

Penelope opened her eyes.

At first, nothing had changed. The clearing was still empty, the air still silent. But then, out of the corner of her eye, she saw something—faint, like a shimmer in the distance. She stepped forward, her heart racing, and as she moved, the shimmer grew stronger.

"There!" she gasped, pointing ahead. "Do you see it?"

Jasper leaned forward on her shoulder, squinting. "I'll be! There it is! It's faint, but I see it!"

The shimmer slowly solidified into a bridge, its outline becoming clearer with each passing second. The bridge seemed to be made of light, delicate and ethereal, stretching across the empty space toward something far off in the distance—a faint, misty outline of what could only be the island. The bridge wasn't made of wood or stone, but something more ephemeral, like starlight woven together into a solid path.

Penelope's heart soared. "It worked! It's really here!"

Jasper let out a whistle. "Well, I'll be! You did it. The invisible bridge."

Without hesitation, Penelope stepped onto the bridge. The moment her foot touched its surface, the shimmering light beneath her feet grew brighter, solidifying into a clear, sturdy path. She took a deep breath and continued walking, her steps slow but confident. The bridge held firm beneath her, though it felt like walking on air.

Jasper clung tightly to her shoulder, his eyes wide as they crossed the vast expanse. "This is unbelievable! We're walking on light!"

Penelope smiled. "I guess we just needed to believe."

The bridge stretched farther than Penelope had expected. As they walked, the island slowly came into view, emerging from the mist that had hung over it like a veil. The island itself was small but lush, covered in dense, emerald-green foliage. Towering trees with twisting, silver trunks lined the shore, their leaves sparkling like gems in the moonlight.

When they reached the other side, Penelope stepped off the bridge and onto the soft, mossy ground. The moment she did, the shimmering light behind them flickered and disappeared, the bridge vanishing as though it had never been there.

"Well, that's a neat trick," Jasper said, hopping down to inspect the island. "I've never seen anything like it."

Penelope looked around, her eyes wide with wonder. The island was alive with magic. The air here felt different, heavier with the scent of ancient wood and fresh earth, as if the place was filled with untold stories. Penelope could feel the presence of something old and powerful, waiting to reveal itself.

"What is this place?" she whispered.

As if in response, the trees rustled, and a soft, melodic sound filled the air. From the shadows of the forest emerged creatures unlike any Penelope had ever seen. They moved gracefully, their bodies slender and tall, their skin shimmering with colors that shifted like the light on the bridge. They had delicate, translucent wings like dragonflies and eyes that gleamed with wisdom.

Jasper's jaw dropped. "Mythical creatures," he whispered. "This island is home to them."

The creatures approached Penelope slowly, their eyes curious but not unfriendly. One of them stepped forward, its voice a soft, musical hum. "You have crossed the bridge of belief," it said, its words flowing like a melody. "Only those who trust in the impossible may set foot on this island."

Penelope nodded, still in awe. "We didn't know if the bridge would appear, but we believed in it."

The creature smiled, its wings fluttering gently. "That belief is what brought you here. This island is hidden from those who do not seek the extraordinary. It is a place where magic thrives, and where the mythical beings of the forest find sanctuary."

Jasper, still wide-eyed, managed to speak. "What kind of place is this? And why is it hidden?"

The creature turned its gaze toward the trees, its expression thoughtful. "This island is a refuge, a place where the creatures of magic can live in peace, away from the eyes of those who would misuse their gifts. It has been hidden for centuries, known only to those who believe in the impossible."

Penelope felt a sense of awe and gratitude. This island was not just a magical place—it was a sanctuary, a place where the forest's most wondrous beings could live freely.

The creature gestured toward the heart of the island, where a path lined with glowing flowers stretched out before them. "Come," it said. "There is much for you to learn here."

With Jasper by her side, Penelope followed the creature down the path, her heart filled with wonder and excitement. The invisible bridge had led them to a world of magic and mystery, and she knew that the island held even more secrets waiting to be uncovered.

Chapter 8: The Island of Dreams

The soft glow of the flowers along the path illuminated Penelope's way as she and Jasper ventured deeper into the island. It was a place unlike any Penelope had ever imagined—a sanctuary for mythical creatures and beings who lived hidden from the rest of the forest. The air was thick with magic, the island alive with a sense of wonder and possibility. Penelope felt as though anything could happen here.

The mythical creatures that had greeted them moved silently through the trees, their translucent wings glimmering in the soft light. Penelope felt no fear, only curiosity. The island had an air of peace, as though it had been untouched by time and the outside world for centuries.

As they walked, one of the creatures—who had introduced itself as Aeris—turned to Penelope, its voice a soft hum. "This island is special," Aeris said. "It exists not just as a place of sanctuary, but as a place of dreams."

Penelope frowned, intrigued. "Dreams?"

Aeris nodded, its delicate wings fluttering. "The Island of Dreams is connected to the dream realm. Here, what you dream can become reality. But you must be careful, for dreams are unpredictable. They can bring wonder or chaos, depending on the heart of the dreamer."

Jasper, perched on Penelope's shoulder, twitched his nose nervously. "Dreams becoming reality? That sounds a bit dangerous."

Aeris smiled softly. "It can be. That is why only those with true control over their dreams may stay here for long. Otherwise, their dreams may spiral out of control, creating things they did not intend."

Penelope felt a flicker of unease. She had always been a vivid dreamer, her imagination running wild even in sleep. The thought of her dreams becoming real both excited and frightened her. She glanced at the enchanted map, which was glowing faintly in her satchel, as if guiding her toward something important.

"What would happen if someone couldn't control their dreams?" Penelope asked, her voice quiet.

Aeris's expression grew more serious. "Then their dreams could become nightmares. The island would reflect their deepest fears, and it would be difficult to return to reality. That is why you must learn to master your dreams while you are here."

Penelope swallowed hard. The thought of her wildest dreams coming to life was both thrilling and daunting. But she had no choice—she needed to learn how to control them, or risk losing herself in a world of chaos.

As they continued walking, Aeris led them to a clearing at the heart of the island. In the center of the clearing was a large, crystal-clear pool, its surface perfectly still. The water reflected the sky above, which was now a deep shade of purple as the sun began to set. Surrounding the pool were tall, white flowers, their petals glowing softly in the fading light.

"This is the Pool of Dreams," Aeris said, gesturing toward the water. "It is where dreamers come to meditate and connect with their inner selves. The pool will show you your dreams, and it will help you learn to control them."

Penelope took a step closer to the pool, her reflection staring back at her from the still water. She knelt down by the edge, feeling a strange pull toward it, as though the pool were calling to her.

"What do I need to do?" she asked, her voice barely a whisper.

Aeris smiled gently. "Close your eyes, and let the pool reveal your dreams. Focus on your heart and mind. You must remain calm and centered, for your emotions will shape what you see."

Penelope nodded, feeling a mixture of excitement and anxiety. She glanced at Jasper, who gave her a reassuring nod, though he looked a bit worried himself.

"You've got this, Penelope," he said. "Just stay focused."

Taking a deep breath, Penelope closed her eyes and allowed her thoughts to drift. She felt the cool air on her skin, the soft rustling of the leaves in the trees, and the gentle hum of magic in the air. Slowly, she let her mind slip into a state of calm, focusing on the stillness of the pool.

At first, nothing happened. The world around her remained quiet and peaceful, and she began to wonder if she was doing something wrong. But then, she felt a subtle shift. The air around her grew warmer, and a faint sound reached her ears—like the soft murmur of voices, distant but familiar.

Penelope opened her eyes.

The pool's surface had changed. Instead of reflecting the sky, it now showed an entirely different scene. Penelope gasped as she realized she was looking at one of her dreams—one she had often had as a child. In the water, she saw a vast field of flowers, their petals glowing with colors she had never seen before. The sky above was a swirling canvas of pink and orange, and in the distance, she could see a large, twisting tree covered in shimmering lights.

"This...this is my dream," Penelope whispered in awe.

Aeris nodded. "The pool reflects the dreams in your heart. But remember, you are not just an observer here. You have the power to shape your dreams."

Penelope stared at the dreamscape in the water, feeling a strange sense of power bubbling up inside her. She could sense the magic of the island merging with her imagination, offering her control over what she saw. Tentatively, she focused on the flowers, imagining them growing taller, their petals opening wider.

To her astonishment, the flowers in the pool's reflection obeyed. They grew and blossomed, their colors shifting and changing as she willed it. The tree in the distance grew larger as well, its branches stretching toward the sky.

"This is incredible," Penelope breathed, her mind racing with possibilities.

But just as she was beginning to feel confident, something changed. The sky in the reflection darkened, the vibrant colors fading into shades of grey. The flowers began to wilt, their petals drooping and turning black. A cold wind swept through the dreamscape, and the twisting tree in the distance seemed to shudder as its branches withered.

Penelope's heart raced as a sense of dread washed over her. She hadn't willed this to happen—it was as though her fears had taken hold, twisting the dream into something dark.

"No!" she cried, panic rising in her chest.

The dreamscape in the pool grew darker still, and Penelope felt the pull of her fear growing stronger. She could hear whispers in the wind, voices calling out to her, growing louder and more menacing.

Jasper leapt to her side, his tiny claws gripping her arm. "Penelope, stay calm! Don't let it take over!"

Penelope squeezed her eyes shut, trying to push the fear away, but it was too strong. The nightmare was spiralling out of control, slipping further and further into darkness.

Aeris's voice cut through the chaos, firm but gentle. "Penelope, you must remember: the power of the dream is in your hands. You control it, not the other way around."

Penelope took a shaky breath, forcing herself to focus. The nightmare was a manifestation of her own fear—her fear of losing control, of being overwhelmed by the magic around her. But it didn't have to be this way.

Slowly, she opened her eyes, her gaze fixed on the pool. The dark clouds still swirled in the sky, and the flowers lay wilted on the ground. But Penelope refused to let the nightmare win. She took a deep breath and focused on the light within her heart—the same light that had guided her through the forest, the same curiosity and wonder that had driven her forward.

"I can do this," she whispered.

She concentrated on the scene in the pool, imagining the clouds parting, the flowers blooming once again. She visualized the darkness fading, replaced by the vibrant colors of her dream. And, little by little, the nightmare began to dissolve. The sky brightened, the flowers lifted their heads, and the twisting tree stood tall and strong once more.

Penelope smiled as the dreamscape transformed, filled with light and beauty once again. She had done it—she had taken control of her dream.

When she looked up, Aeris was smiling at her, a look of quiet approval in its eyes. "Well done, Penelope. You have learned the most important lesson of the Island of Dreams: you are the master of your own mind."

Penelope stood up, her heart lighter than it had been moments before. She had faced her fear and come out stronger for it.

"Thank you," she said softly.

Jasper, who had been watching with wide eyes, let out a sigh of relief. "Well, that was intense. But you did it, Penelope! You controlled the dream!"

Penelope smiled. "I couldn't have done it without you reminding me to stay calm."

Aeris stepped forward, its wings shimmering in the soft light of the clearing. "The Island of Dreams has given you a gift, Penelope. The ability to control your dreams is not something everyone possesses. It will serve you well on your journey."

Penelope nodded, feeling a sense of confidence settle over her. She knew now that she could face whatever challenges lay ahead, whether they were born of magic or her own imagination.

As they left the clearing, Penelope glanced back at the Pool of Dreams, its surface once again still and clear. She knew that the island had more to teach her, but she also knew she was ready for whatever came next.

With Jasper by her side and the enchanted map still glowing softly in her satchel, Penelope set off toward the next part of her adventure, her heart filled with wonder and determination.

Chapter 9: The Friendly Giant

The sky was beginning to shift from bright blue to the soft hues of dusk as Penelope and Jasper made their way through the dense forest, following the ever-glowing map. Their previous adventure on the Island of Dreams had left Penelope feeling empowered, having learned to control her imagination and fears. Now, as they ventured toward the next destination on the map, they entered a region where the forest began to thin, the ground sloping gently upward.

"We're heading toward the mountains," Penelope noted as she traced the glowing lines on the map, which showed a winding path leading into high, rocky terrain. "Look at these markings." She pointed to a large symbol near the top of the map: a towering figure drawn in soft, curving lines. It was unlike anything she had seen before on her journey.

"Looks like we're about to meet someone big," Jasper said, peering at the map. "Let's just hope they're friendly."

Penelope chuckled, though she felt a small flicker of anxiety. "I hope so too."

The two continued walking as the landscape changed. The trees gradually gave way to towering rocks and steep cliffs, and soon, the forest had vanished completely, replaced by craggy mountain paths and rugged terrain. The air grew colder, and a gentle breeze blew through the rocks, carrying with it the scent of pine and mountain air. In the distance, Penelope could see the jagged peaks of the mountains rising into the clouds, their tops dusted with snow.

"I didn't realize we were so close to the mountains," Penelope said, her breath fogging in the cool air. "I wonder who lives up here."

Jasper, who had hopped onto a nearby rock, squinted into the distance. "We'll find out soon enough. But if that map is any indication, we're about to meet someone...giant."

As they climbed higher, Penelope felt a strange sense of anticipation. The glowing map had led her to so many magical places, each one more wondrous than the last. But something about the symbol of the towering figure intrigued her. It felt different, more personal somehow.

After what felt like hours of climbing, the path led them into a wide, open plateau nestled between two towering peaks. Penelope paused, catching her breath as she looked around. The plateau was peaceful and quiet, the rocky cliffs casting long shadows across the ground. In the distance, the sun was beginning to set, casting a golden glow over the mountains.

But something about the place felt lonely. Penelope could sense it in the air—a deep, aching sadness that seemed to hang over the plateau like a weight. She glanced at Jasper, who had fallen unusually quiet.

"Do you feel that?" Penelope asked softly.

Jasper nodded, his eyes scanning the cliffs. "Yeah. It's like...something's missing."

Penelope was about to speak again when she heard a sound—soft at first, but growing louder with each passing moment. It was the sound of heavy footsteps, the ground trembling slightly beneath her feet. Penelope's heart raced as she turned toward the source of the sound.

Emerging from behind a towering rock was the largest creature Penelope had ever seen.

It was a giant—a true giant, standing at least twenty feet tall, with broad shoulders and a long, flowing beard that reached down to its chest. Its skin was the color of the earth, a warm, weathered brown, and its eyes—large and kind—gleamed with a soft, golden light. The giant's expression was not fierce or menacing, but rather filled with a deep, quiet sadness.

Penelope gasped, her heart pounding in her chest. The giant's sheer size was overwhelming, but there was something gentle about him, something that made her feel safe rather than afraid.

The giant paused when he saw Penelope and Jasper, his eyes widening in surprise. He took a slow step forward, his massive hands hanging by his sides, and when he spoke, his voice was deep and rumbling, like the sound of distant thunder.

"Hello there, little ones," the giant said, his voice gentle despite his size. "What brings you to these lonely mountains?"

Penelope swallowed hard, trying to find her voice. "We...we were following a map," she said, holding up the glowing parchment. "It led us here."

The giant's eyes softened, and he knelt down, bringing himself closer to Penelope's level. Even on his knees, he was still several times her height, but his presence was not threatening. "Ah, I see," the giant said, his voice tinged with a wistful note. "The map brought you here. It must have known that I was in need of company."

Jasper, who had been silent up until now, leapt onto Penelope's shoulder and spoke up. "Company? Have you been living up here alone?"

The giant nodded slowly, his large eyes filled with sadness. "For many, many years," he said. "I once had friends—other giants who lived in these mountains—but over time, they left. Some went in search of adventure, others faded away into the mists of time. I stayed here, waiting...hoping that one day, someone might come and visit me. But no one ever does."

Penelope's heart ached for the giant. She could feel the loneliness radiating from him, the weight of centuries spent in isolation. "That must be so hard," she said softly. "Being all alone for so long."

The giant gave a sad smile. "It is. The mountains are beautiful, but they are quiet. And quiet can be lonely, especially when there is no one to share it with."

Penelope took a step closer, her fear melting away completely. "Well, you're not alone anymore. We're here now."

The giant's eyes brightened at her words, and for the first time, Penelope saw a flicker of hope in his expression. "You...you would stay? Even just for a little while?"

Jasper nodded enthusiastically. "Of course! You seem like a friendly enough fellow, and we could all use some company. Right, Penelope?"

Penelope smiled. "Absolutely. I'd love to hear about the mountains and your life here."

The giant's smile grew wider, and for the first time, he looked genuinely happy. "That would mean more to me than you know," he said, his voice thick with emotion. "Please, come. Let me show you my home."

With that, the giant led Penelope and Jasper deeper into the plateau, where a small, peaceful clearing lay nestled between the cliffs. The giant's home was simple—a large stone cave built into the side of the mountain, with a cozy fire crackling near the entrance. Despite the size of the cave, it felt warm and inviting, filled with simple comforts like woven blankets and stone carvings.

"This is my home," the giant said, gesturing to the cave. "I've lived here for many years, but I haven't had guests in a very long time."

Penelope marvelled at the giant's craftsmanship. The cave walls were adorned with intricate carvings, each one telling a story of the giant's life. There were scenes of towering mountains, vast forests, and even other giants, their faces etched with kindness and strength.

"These are beautiful," Penelope said, running her hand over one of the carvings. "Did you make them yourself?"

The giant nodded. "Yes. It was my way of remembering the friends I once had. Each carving represents a memory, a story from long ago."

Penelope felt a lump rise in her throat. She couldn't imagine being alone for so many years, surrounded only by memories of the past. "You're not alone anymore," she said softly, looking up at the giant. "We're here, and we're your friends now."

The giant's eyes filled with tears, and he knelt down beside Penelope, his massive hand resting gently on the ground beside her. "Thank you, Penelope," he said, his voice filled with gratitude. "I cannot tell you how much it means to me to hear those words."

Jasper, ever the curious one, hopped down from Penelope's shoulder and scampered over to the fire. "So, do you have any stories to share? Giants must have some pretty epic tales."

The giant chuckled, the sound deep and warm. "Oh, I have plenty of stories, little one. Would you like to hear about the time I saved an entire village from an avalanche?"

Penelope's eyes lit up. "Yes, please! That sounds amazing!"

And so, as the sun set behind the mountains and the stars began to twinkle in the night sky, the giant told them stories—tales of adventure, bravery, and friendship. The fire crackled warmly, and the air was filled with the sound of laughter and the magic of shared stories.

For the first time in centuries, the giant was no longer alone.

Chapter 10: The Cursed Cavern

Penelope and Jasper continued their journey after bidding a fond farewell to the gentle giant. The enchanted map had revealed their next destination: a dark cavern nestled deep within the mountains. The symbol on the map—a jagged, ominous shape—gave Penelope an uneasy feeling. The glowing lines seemed to pulse with a faint, sinister energy, unlike the warm, welcoming light that had guided her to other places in the forest.

"'Cursed Cavern,' huh?" Jasper muttered as he perched on Penelope's shoulder, eyeing the map warily. "Sounds like the kind of place you avoid, not walk into."

Penelope nodded, a chill running down her spine. "I know. But the map is leading us there for a reason. There's something we need to find or fix. Maybe breaking the curse will help us get one step closer to the Sanctuary."

Jasper scratched his head. "Well, whatever's waiting for us, I'm sure we can handle it. I just hope it's not, you know...shadow monsters."

Penelope gave him a nervous smile. "Let's hope not."

The path to the cavern was treacherous, winding through rocky terrain and narrow cliffs. As they approached, the air grew colder, and a strange, heavy silence settled over the mountains. Even the birds and wildlife seemed to avoid this place, leaving the area eerily still.

The entrance to the cavern loomed ahead—a gaping hole in the side of the mountain, its edges jagged and sharp, like the mouth of a giant beast. The darkness inside seemed to swallow the light, and as Penelope peered into it, she felt the weight of an unseen presence pressing down on her.

"This is it," Penelope said, her voice barely a whisper.

Jasper shivered, his tail flicking nervously. "I don't like this place, Penelope. There's something...wrong about it."

Penelope took a deep breath, steeling herself. She felt the same unease, but she knew they couldn't turn back now. There was something inside that needed to be confronted. "We have to face it," she said, her voice firmer. "Whatever's in there, we'll deal with it together."

With that, Penelope stepped into the cavern, her heart pounding in her chest. The moment she crossed the threshold, the temperature dropped even further, and the shadows seemed to thicken, curling around the walls like tendrils of smoke. Jasper clung tightly to her shoulder, his tiny claws digging into her shirt.

The cavern walls were rough and damp, the air thick with the scent of earth and stone. Penelope could hear the faint drip of water echoing through the darkness, but other than that, it was eerily silent. The deeper they went, the more oppressive the atmosphere became, as if the very air was weighed down by the curse that plagued this place.

And then, Penelope saw them—the shadows.

At first, they seemed like nothing more than natural darkness cast by the jagged walls of the cavern. But as Penelope's eyes adjusted to the gloom, she realized they were moving. The shadows stretched and writhed along the walls, twisting into shapes that seemed almost alive.

Jasper froze on her shoulder. "Penelope...do you see that?"

Penelope nodded, her heart racing. "Yes."

The shadows moved in unnatural ways, slithering and creeping along the ground, flickering like candle flames caught in a breeze. Some of them formed shapes that resembled figures—humanoid, but distorted, their limbs too long and their movements jerky and unnatural.

Penelope took a step back, her breath catching in her throat. She had never seen anything like this before. These weren't just ordinary shadows; they were alive, and they were watching her.

One of the shadowy figures detached itself from the wall and slithered toward her, its shape flickering and shifting as it moved.

Penelope's heart pounded as the shadow loomed in front of her, its formless face hovering inches away from hers. For a moment, she thought it might attack, but then it simply hovered there, as if waiting for something.

"What do we do?" Jasper whispered, his voice trembling.

Penelope swallowed hard. "I don't know."

The shadow seemed to sense her fear, its shape growing larger and more menacing as it fed on her anxiety. Penelope could feel the darkness pressing in on her, the weight of the curse bearing down on her shoulders. She felt trapped, surrounded by shadows that seemed to grow stronger the more afraid she became.

But then, Penelope remembered what Aeris had told her on the Island of Dreams. She had learned how to control her dreams, to face her fears and overcome them. Maybe this was the same. Maybe the shadows weren't as powerful as they seemed—maybe they were feeding off her fear, growing stronger because she was afraid.

Penelope closed her eyes and took a deep breath, willing herself to remain calm. She had faced many dangers in this forest, and each time, she had found a way to overcome them. The shadows were frightening, yes, but she couldn't let her fear control her.

"Penelope, what are you doing?" Jasper asked, his voice tinged with panic.

"I'm not afraid," Penelope whispered, more to herself than to Jasper. "I'm not afraid of them."

She opened her eyes and stared directly at the shadow in front of her. Its form flickered, its shape twisting and changing as if trying to intimidate her. But Penelope stood her ground, refusing to let it control her. She took another step forward, her gaze steady.

"I'm not afraid of you," she said, her voice clear and strong. "You can't control me."

For a moment, nothing happened. The shadow hovered in front of her, its form flickering uncertainly. And then, slowly, it began to shrink. The darkness that had surrounded Penelope started to recede, the weight of the curse lifting as her fear dissolved.

The other shadows along the walls began to shrink as well, their forms losing their menacing shapes. The more Penelope faced her fear, the weaker the shadows became, until they were nothing more than faint wisps of darkness clinging to the walls.

Penelope took a deep breath, relief flooding through her. "We did it," she whispered.

Jasper let out a shaky laugh. "I can't believe that worked. You stared down the shadows!"

Penelope smiled. "I think they were feeding off my fear. Once I stopped being afraid, they lost their power."

With the shadows weakened, Penelope and Jasper continued deeper into the cavern. The air felt lighter now, the oppressive atmosphere fading as the curse began to lift. As they reached the heart of the cavern, they found what they had been searching for.

In the center of the chamber stood an ancient stone altar, covered in dust and cobwebs. Atop the altar lay a small, glowing object—a pendant shaped like a crescent moon. The pendant pulsed with a soft, silver light, its glow casting faint shadows on the walls.

"This must be the source of the curse," Penelope said, stepping closer to the altar.

Jasper nodded. "Looks like it. What do you think we should do with it?"

Penelope reached out and gently picked up the pendant. The moment her fingers touched the cool metal, a wave of warmth washed over her, and the remaining shadows in the cavern dissolved into nothingness. The curse was broken.

She held the pendant in her hand, feeling the magic within it. It was a powerful object, but it no longer held any darkness. The curse had been lifted, and the shadows were gone.

Penelope tucked the pendant into her satchel, knowing that it would be important later on in her journey. As they turned to leave the cavern, Jasper let out a sigh of relief.

"Well, that was terrifying," he said, hopping onto her shoulder. "But we made it through. You were amazing, Penelope."

Penelope smiled, feeling a sense of accomplishment. "I couldn't have done it without you, Jasper."

As they stepped out of the cavern and back into the fresh mountain air, Penelope felt lighter, as though a weight had been lifted from her shoulders. The cursed cavern was no longer a place of darkness and fear, and she had faced one of her deepest challenges.

With the pendant safely in her possession and the shadows behind them, Penelope and Jasper set off once more, their hearts full of hope for the next leg of their adventure.

Chapter 11: The Secret of the Owl

The journey through the forest had taken Penelope and Jasper to many wondrous and sometimes terrifying places, but as they ventured farther from the Cursed Cavern, a sense of peace settled over them. The air was warmer, and the trees grew tall and straight, their leaves whispering softly in the breeze. Penelope could feel the magic of the forest all around her, like a soft hum beneath the surface of everything.

The enchanted map had once again shifted, its glowing lines leading them toward a new destination. This time, the map was marked with the image of an owl, its wings spread wide as though soaring through the sky. There were no paths marked, only a deep thicket of trees surrounding a clearing in the distance.

Jasper sat perched on Penelope's shoulder, his tiny paws gripping her sleeve as he peered at the map. "An owl, huh? Wise creatures, owls. Always full of riddles and ancient knowledge. Let's just hope this one's in the mood to talk."

Penelope smiled. "I'm sure it will be. The map wouldn't lead us here if it didn't want us to find something important."

They followed the glowing lines of the map deeper into the forest, the trees growing denser around them. The air was thick with the scent of pine and rich earth, and the only sounds were the soft rustling of leaves and the occasional chirp of birds. As they approached the heart of the forest, Penelope noticed a change in the atmosphere. The air felt heavier, as if the forest itself was watching them, waiting for something.

Finally, they arrived at a small clearing, just as the map had shown. At the center of the clearing stood a single, towering tree, its bark ancient and gnarled. The tree's branches stretched high into the sky, and nestled among them, barely visible in the fading light, was a large, shadowy figure.

Penelope squinted up at the tree. "Do you see that?"

Jasper followed her gaze and nodded. "There it is—the owl."

The owl, perched on one of the highest branches, was enormous. Its feathers were a deep shade of brown, flecked with silver that shimmered in the dim light. Its eyes, large and golden, gleamed with intelligence, and its sharp beak was curved into a thoughtful expression. The owl was clearly no ordinary creature—it radiated an ancient wisdom, as though it had been watching over the forest for centuries.

Penelope took a cautious step forward. "Hello?" she called softly.

The owl's head swivelled slowly, its golden eyes locking onto Penelope with a gaze that felt almost too intense. For a moment, the clearing was silent, and then the owl spoke, its voice deep and melodic, like the wind through the trees.

"Who enters my domain?" the owl asked, its eyes narrowing slightly. "What seeker of knowledge dares approach the Watcher of the Forest?"

Penelope swallowed hard, her heart pounding. "My name is Penelope Pine," she said, her voice steady despite her nerves. "I'm on a journey through the forest, and the map led me here. I...I think I'm meant to learn something from you."

The owl studied her for a long moment, its golden eyes unblinking. Then, with a great sweep of its wings, it descended from the branch, landing gracefully on the ground in front of Penelope. Its size was even more imposing up close, but there was no malice in its gaze, only curiosity and a quiet wisdom.

"I see," the owl said, its voice thoughtful. "The forest has chosen you as a seeker, then. Few are guided to my tree. Fewer still leave with the answers they seek."

Jasper, who had been nervously silent up until now, piped up from Penelope's shoulder. "Answers? What kind of answers? We've been looking for all sorts of things—hidden places, magical objects. Are you going to tell us some great secret?"

The owl tilted its head, regarding Jasper with amusement. "I do not give answers freely, little one. Knowledge is earned through understanding, and understanding comes from asking the right questions."

Penelope felt a flicker of excitement. "What questions should I ask?"

The owl's eyes glinted. "That is for you to decide, child. But I will offer you this—three riddles. Solve them, and you may ask one question, and I will answer truthfully. Fail, and you shall leave this place none the wiser."

Penelope's heart raced. Riddles. She had always loved them, the way they twisted logic and forced her to think in new ways. But she knew these wouldn't be simple puzzles—they would require every ounce of her concentration and wit.

"I accept," Penelope said, her voice firm.

The owl nodded slowly, its feathers ruffling as it shifted its weight. "Very well. Listen closely."

The first riddle came, spoken in the owl's deep, rhythmic voice:

"I have no wings, yet I can fly,

I have no eyes, yet all can see me.

I have no voice, yet I speak to you.

What am I?"

Penelope frowned, thinking hard. No wings, but it can fly. No eyes, but it can be seen. No voice, but it speaks... She turned the words over in her mind, searching for the answer.

Jasper whispered in her ear, "Any ideas?"

Penelope's eyes lit up as the answer struck her. "The wind," she said confidently. "It flies without wings, we can feel it even though it has no eyes, and it speaks to us in whispers."

The owl's eyes gleamed with approval. "Correct," it said. "You are clever, seeker. Now, for the second riddle."

The owl ruffled its feathers and spoke again:

"I am not alive, but I can grow.

I have no lungs, but I need air.

What am I?"

Penelope bit her lip, her mind racing. Not alive, but it can grow...no lungs, but it needs air... She thought about things in nature, things that behaved in strange ways. And then it hit her.

"Fire," she said. "It's not alive, but it grows when fed, and it needs air to keep burning."

The owl's expression softened slightly, a hint of admiration in its golden eyes. "You are correct once again, Penelope Pine. Now, for the final riddle. Be cautious, for this one is not so easily answered."

The owl's voice grew softer, more mysterious, as it spoke the final riddle:

"The more you take, the more you leave behind.

What am I?"

Penelope frowned deeply, the riddle echoing in her mind. It was different from the others—more abstract, harder to pin down. The more you take, the more you leave behind. What could it mean?

Jasper was silent, clearly stumped as well.

Penelope closed her eyes, letting the riddle swirl in her mind. The more you take, the more you leave behind. Something that grows the more you interact with it. It's not something physical... She thought of footsteps, the way you leave a trail behind as you walk. The more steps you take, the more footprints you leave behind.

Penelope's eyes flew open. "Footsteps," she said quietly. "The more you take, the more footsteps you leave behind."

The owl's golden eyes gleamed with satisfaction. "You are wise beyond your years, Penelope Pine. Few have answered all my riddles so swiftly."

Penelope let out a breath she hadn't realized she'd been holding. "Does that mean I can ask my question?"

The owl nodded solemnly. "Yes. Ask wisely, for the knowledge you seek may change the course of your journey."

Penelope hesitated. She had so many questions—about the forest, about the Sanctuary, about the magic that had led her here. But there was one question that weighed more heavily than the rest, one that had lingered in her mind since the beginning of her journey.

"What is the true nature of this forest?" Penelope asked, her voice soft but determined. "Where does its magic come from?"

The owl's gaze softened, as though it had expected this question. It spread its wings wide, and the wind stirred the leaves around them, carrying with it the ancient wisdom of the forest.

"The magic of this forest is ancient, older than time itself," the owl said. "It was born from the dreams of the first beings who walked this land, long before humans, before creatures of the earth. The trees, the water, the air—all were shaped by the imagination of the world itself. This forest is not just a place of magic; it is magic. It is alive, ever-changing, responding to the hearts and minds of those who walk within it."

Penelope's breath caught in her throat. "The forest is alive?"

"Yes," the owl replied. "It is a living entity, one that listens, one that watches, one that shapes itself according to the dreams, hopes, and fears of those who dwell within it. The magic you encounter here is not separate from you—it is a reflection of your own inner world."

Penelope's mind raced as she absorbed the owl's words. The forest wasn't just a place—it was a living, breathing thing, shaped by the very people who walked through it. Every wonder, every danger, every secret was a manifestation of the forest's connection to its visitors.

The owl stepped back, folding its wings gently. "Your journey through this forest is far from over, Penelope Pine. But now you understand what lies at its heart. Use this knowledge wisely, for it will guide you to the Sanctuary and beyond."

Penelope nodded, her heart full of wonder and awe. "Thank you," she whispered. "I'll remember your words."

With a final nod, the owl spread its massive wings and soared back into the branches of the ancient tree, disappearing into the shadows.

Penelope stood in silence for a moment, her mind spinning with everything she had learned. The forest was alive, and its magic was tied to her own inner world. It was both beautiful and terrifying, and Penelope knew that her journey had only just begun.

"Come on, Jasper," Penelope said softly. "We have a lot more to discover."

Jasper nodded, still processing what they had just learned. "No kidding. This forest is a whole lot deeper than I thought."

With the owl's riddles solved and the secrets of the forest now partially revealed, Penelope and Jasper set off once more, the enchanted map glowing faintly in her hand. The forest was alive, and its mysteries were waiting for her to uncover them.

Chapter 12: The River of Time

The forest grew quiet as Penelope and Jasper ventured further into its depths, the newly acquired knowledge from the owl weighing heavily on Penelope's mind. The idea that the forest was alive, connected to her and shaped by the thoughts and emotions of its visitors, both fascinated and unsettled her. Each step through the enchanted woods felt different now, as though the trees, the air, even the light around her were more alive, more aware.

But there was little time to dwell on that mystery. The map had shifted again, revealing their next destination—a flowing river, its shimmering waters marked with an ancient symbol of a clock face. The name that appeared on the map was simple, yet mysterious: The River of Time.

Jasper, always curious, peeked at the map from Penelope's shoulder. "A river that flows backward in time? Now that sounds like an adventure! I've heard whispers about such places, but never thought we'd find one."

Penelope smiled but couldn't help feeling a nervous excitement. The idea of seeing time itself unfold before her was exhilarating. What stories would the river reveal? What ancient civilizations had once roamed these lands? She hoped to find answers to the questions swirling in her mind.

They continued walking through the dense forest, the path becoming less defined the deeper they went. The air felt cooler, and the trees became taller and more ancient, their roots twisting beneath the earth like the fingers of time itself. As they neared their destination, a faint sound reached Penelope's ears—the soft, rhythmic murmur of running water.

"There it is," she whispered, her heart quickening.

The River of Time came into view as they stepped through a thicket of trees. It was a narrow, winding river, but its water shimmered strangely, as though it was made of liquid starlight. The surface was smooth and clear, but there was an ethereal quality to it, like something that didn't quite belong in the present. The river flowed steadily, but as Penelope watched it, she realized something extraordinary—the river wasn't moving forward. It was flowing backward.

Jasper's eyes widened. "Well, I'll be. The river really is flowing in reverse!"

Penelope approached the edge of the riverbank, her eyes fixed on the shimmering water. As she knelt down and dipped her fingers into the river, a strange sensation washed over her. The water was cool, but instead of feeling like any ordinary river, it felt as if time itself was slipping through her fingers—moments, memories, and stories all flowing past her, moving backward through history.

"I can feel it," Penelope whispered, awe in her voice. "It's like the river is carrying the past with it."

Jasper tilted his head, clearly fascinated. "So, what happens if we follow it? Do we...see the past?"

Penelope nodded, standing up. "I think so. The river flows backward in time, so maybe if we walk along its banks, we'll see the history of this place. Maybe even the origins of the forest."

With that thought, Penelope began to walk along the riverbank, following the shimmering water as it wound through the trees. The further they walked, the stranger the world around them became. The air grew heavier, as though the weight of time itself was pressing down on them. And then, slowly at first, the forest began to change.

The trees shifted, growing taller and more vibrant. The underbrush thickened, and Penelope could hear the faint sounds of voices, carried on the wind. The river continued to flow backward, and with it, the forest around them seemed to transform, taking them further and further into the past.

Suddenly, Penelope gasped. Up ahead, where the river curved gently around a bend, she saw them—people. But not like the villagers from Windy Hollow or the other forest travellers she had encountered. These people were dressed in simple, ancient clothing, their faces lined with the wisdom and hardship of a time long forgotten.

Jasper clung to Penelope's shoulder, his voice barely a whisper. "Are we...are we seeing the past?"

Penelope nodded, her eyes wide with wonder. The figures ahead were tending to the land, gathering plants, and speaking in a language Penelope didn't understand. Yet there was a familiarity to them, as though these were the people who had once been deeply connected to the forest.

"This must be one of the ancient civilizations that lived here," Penelope whispered. "The ones who shaped the forest with their dreams."

The river flowed onward, and as Penelope and Jasper continued to follow it, the scenes before them changed. The forest grew even wilder, more untamed, and the people they saw became fewer, their presence fading as the land became overgrown. Penelope realized that they were moving further back in time, watching as the ancient civilization slowly disappeared, leaving the forest to reclaim the land.

And then, the river's path opened into a wide clearing, and Penelope stopped in her tracks. Before her stood an enormous stone structure, half hidden beneath the thick vines and trees that had grown over it. The structure was clearly ancient, its stone walls carved with intricate patterns and symbols that seemed to pulse with a faint, lingering magic.

"This...this is a temple," Penelope said, awe filling her voice. "It must have been built by the first people of the forest."

Jasper hopped down from her shoulder, approaching the temple with wide eyes. "It looks like it's been here for centuries, maybe even longer. Do you think it's connected to the magic of the forest?"

Penelope nodded slowly. "It must be. The owl said that the forest was born from the dreams of the first beings who lived here. Maybe this temple was where they came to connect with the forest's magic."

She stepped closer to the temple, her hand brushing against the cool stone. The carvings were intricate, depicting strange creatures, ancient symbols, and scenes of people interacting with the land in ways Penelope had never seen before. It was as though the temple held the key to understanding the forest's true origins.

But as Penelope's fingers traced the carvings, a strange sensation washed over her. The air around her grew still, and the world seemed to shift. Suddenly, the scene before her changed again, and she found herself standing in the middle of the clearing, but it was no longer abandoned.

The temple was alive with activity. People—hundreds of them—moved around her, their voices filling the air as they worked together to build and shape the land. The forest around them was vibrant and full of life, and Penelope could feel the magic pulsing in the air, thick and powerful.

"This...this is what the forest used to be," Penelope whispered, her heart racing. "This is the past."

Jasper, who had been staring in wide-eyed amazement, turned to Penelope. "We're seeing how it all began."

The people of the ancient civilization worked with the forest, not against it. They shaped the trees, the rivers, and the earth, using their dreams and their magic to create a place of harmony and wonder. The temple was at the center of it all, a place where the people came to offer their dreams to the forest, to keep the magic alive.

But then, slowly, Penelope saw the change.

The people began to fade. One by one, they left the temple, leaving the land to grow wild and untamed. The forest began to reclaim what had once been shaped by human hands, and the magic that had once pulsed so strongly began to weaken.

Penelope's heart ached as she watched the ancient civilization fade into memory, their connection to the forest slipping away. "Why did they leave?" she whispered, more to herself than to Jasper.

But before she could dwell on the question, the scene around her shifted again, and the temple was once more a forgotten ruin, hidden deep within the forest. The people were gone, and the magic of the land had become distant, waiting for someone to rediscover it.

Penelope stood in silence, the weight of what she had seen pressing down on her. The River of Time had shown her the forest's past, its connection to the people who had once lived here. They had been the keepers of the forest's magic, but over time, they had disappeared, leaving the land to grow wild and forgotten.

Jasper broke the silence, his voice soft. "Do you think the forest is still waiting for them to come back?"

Penelope shook her head slowly. "No. I think the forest is waiting for someone new to understand its magic. Someone who can bring that connection back."

As she looked out over the river, Penelope knew that her journey through the forest was far from over. The River of Time had shown her the past, but the future was still unwritten. And perhaps, just perhaps, it was up to her to help restore the connection that had been lost so long ago.

"We need to keep moving," Penelope said, her voice filled with quiet determination. "There's still so much more to uncover."

With the vision of the past still fresh in her mind, Penelope and Jasper turned away from the river and continued their journey, the forest around them alive with the echoes of history and the promise of what was yet to come.

Chapter 13: The Butterfly Kingdom

After their journey along the River of Time, Penelope and Jasper found themselves walking through a part of the forest that was alive with color. Bright flowers bloomed in every direction, their petals glowing in the soft sunlight, and the air was thick with the sweet scent of nectar. Butterflies flitted from flower to flower, their wings shimmering in shades of blue, purple, and gold.

"This place is beautiful," Penelope said, her eyes wide with wonder as she watched the butterflies dance through the air. "It feels like something out of a dream."

Jasper, who was perched on her shoulder, nodded. "It's a nice change of pace from cursed caverns and shadowy forests, that's for sure."

As they continued walking, Penelope noticed something strange. The butterflies seemed to be moving with a purpose, flying in the same direction, as though they were following an invisible path. She paused, watching the swarm of butterflies as they fluttered through the trees, and a curious feeling settled over her.

"Look at them," Penelope said, pointing toward the fluttering mass. "They're all heading in the same direction. Do you think they're going somewhere?"

Jasper cocked his head, watching the butterflies as well. "Maybe. There's definitely something odd about it."

Penelope's curiosity got the better of her. She followed the trail of butterflies, weaving through the trees and tall grasses until she reached the edge of a hidden meadow. There, at the center of the meadow, stood something she had never seen before.

It was a castle, but not like any castle Penelope had ever imagined. The walls were made of twisting vines and flowers, their colors changing with every breeze. The towers rose high into the sky, their spires adorned with shimmering petals. And surrounding the castle, fluttering through the air like tiny, colorful sentinels, were thousands of butterflies.

"This...this is incredible," Penelope whispered in awe. "It's like a kingdom made entirely of butterflies."

Jasper blinked in disbelief. "I didn't even know butterflies could build castles. We've got to check this out!"

Penelope moved cautiously toward the castle, the butterflies parting to let her pass. As she approached, the air around her seemed to shimmer, and the sound of fluttering wings filled the air like a soft, musical hum.

"Hello?" Penelope called, unsure if anyone—or anything—would respond.

To her surprise, the butterflies suddenly began to gather in front of her, swirling together in a bright, colorful cloud. Slowly, the cloud of butterflies began to take shape, forming the outline of a tall, regal figure. The butterflies settled into place, their wings shimmering as they created the image of a queen with delicate, iridescent wings.

"Welcome, traveller," the butterfly queen said, her voice soft and melodic. "You have found the Butterfly Kingdom, a place of peace and beauty."

Penelope's eyes widened. "The Butterfly Kingdom? I've never heard of it before."

The queen's wings fluttered gently. "Few have. We have kept ourselves hidden from the rest of the world, living in harmony with the forest. But I fear that our time may be coming to an end."

Penelope frowned, her heart sinking. "What do you mean? What's happening?"

The queen's form flickered for a moment, as though the butterflies were struggling to maintain the shape. "A dark force has entered the forest," she explained. "It is spreading through the land, corrupting everything it touches. Even the magic that sustains our kingdom is beginning to fade. If something is not done soon, the Butterfly Kingdom will disappear."

Penelope's heart raced. She had seen many strange and magical things in the forest, but the thought of an entire kingdom of butterflies being wiped out was heartbreaking. She couldn't let that happen.

"There has to be something we can do," Penelope said, determination filling her voice. "We'll help you stop this force."

The queen's eyes, made of thousands of tiny, fluttering wings, glimmered with gratitude. "Your offer of help is kind, but the darkness is powerful. It spreads like a shadow, slowly draining the life from everything it touches. The butterflies of the kingdom have tried to resist it, but we are not strong enough on our own."

Penelope glanced at Jasper, who nodded in agreement. "We've faced darkness before," he said. "We'll do whatever we can."

The queen gestured toward the heart of the meadow, where a large, ancient tree stood. Its branches were covered in vines, but the leaves at its base had turned black, the bark twisted and sickly. The tree, which had once been the source of life and magic for the Butterfly Kingdom, was now withering.

"This tree is the heart of our kingdom," the queen said. "Its magic sustains us. But as you can see, it is dying. The dark force has already begun to consume it."

Penelope took a step closer, her brow furrowed as she examined the tree. She could feel the magic pulsing weakly from its roots, like a fading heartbeat. Whatever darkness was spreading through the forest, it was choking the life out of everything it touched.

"Is there a way to reverse the damage?" Penelope asked, her mind racing. "Maybe we can heal the tree, or stop the darkness from spreading."

The queen's wings fluttered weakly. "There is one way," she said slowly. "Deep in the forest, beyond the hills, there is a flower—the Lumen Blossom. It is said to hold the power to restore life and drive away darkness. But the journey to find it is dangerous. The dark force has already begun to corrupt the land around it."

Penelope clenched her fists, determination flaring within her. "We'll find the Lumen Blossom," she said firmly. "We'll bring it back and save the tree—and your kingdom."

The queen's eyes shone with hope, but there was also a sadness in her voice. "It will not be easy, but we have no other choice. Without the Lumen Blossom, the Butterfly Kingdom will fade, and our world will be lost forever."

Penelope felt a weight settle on her shoulders. The butterflies—so fragile, yet so beautiful—depended on her now. She couldn't let them down. She had already seen so many incredible things on this journey, and she knew that the forest's magic ran deep. If there was a way to save the kingdom, she would find it.

Jasper, ever the optimist, gave Penelope a confident nod. "We've faced worse, right? What's a little dark force compared to all the things we've seen? Let's get that flower and save the day."

The queen spread her wings, the butterflies composing her body shimmering in the light. "Thank you, Penelope Pine. You carry with you the spirit of kindness and courage. May the wind guide your path and protect you."

With a deep breath, Penelope turned toward the dark forest beyond the meadow, where the Lumen Blossom awaited. The path ahead would not be easy, but with Jasper by her side and the fate of the Butterfly Kingdom resting on her shoulders, she knew she had to be brave.

The butterflies flitted around her as she and Jasper left the meadow, their wings glowing softly in the fading light. The once-peaceful kingdom was now in grave danger, but Penelope was determined to bring hope back to the fragile, beautiful creatures who called it home.

As they ventured into the shadows of the forest, the air grew cooler, and the light around them dimmed. The trees here were twisted and blackened, their leaves withered and lifeless. The darkness was creeping through the land, corrupting everything in its path.

But Penelope's heart was strong. She had seen the beauty of the Butterfly Kingdom, and she knew what was at stake. The Lumen Blossom held the power to restore the light, and she would find it—no matter what stood in her way.

With determination in her step and the knowledge that she was fighting for something greater than herself, Penelope set off toward her next great challenge.

Chapter 14: The Singing Stones

The forest beyond the Butterfly Kingdom had grown darker, the trees twisted and gnarled as the corruption from the dark force spread through the land. Penelope and Jasper pressed on, determined to find the Lumen Blossom and save the Butterfly Kingdom. As they ventured deeper into the shadows, a strange, enchanting sound reached Penelope's ears—a soft, haunting melody that seemed to come from nowhere and everywhere all at once.

Penelope stopped in her tracks, tilting her head to listen. The sound was unlike anything she had ever heard before. It was beautiful, yet sad, a song that echoed through the trees and wrapped around her like a whispered secret.

"Do you hear that?" Penelope asked softly, her voice barely above a whisper.

Jasper's ears perked up. "Yeah, I hear it. What is that?"

Penelope shook her head. "I don't know. But it's coming from up ahead. Let's go see."

Drawn by the ethereal music, Penelope followed the sound through the forest, winding her way between ancient trees and thick underbrush. The closer she got, the stronger the melody became, filling the air with its haunting beauty.

After a few moments, Penelope emerged into a small clearing. At the center of the clearing stood a circle of large stones, each one covered in intricate carvings that glowed faintly in the dim light. The stones were arranged in a perfect circle, and it was from these stones that the music seemed to be emanating. The stones weren't just silent monuments—they were singing.

Penelope's breath caught in her throat. The melody was so beautiful, so mesmerizing, that for a moment, all she could do was stand and listen. The music rose and fell like the wind, each note clear and pure, as though the stones themselves were alive with ancient magic.

Jasper hopped down from her shoulder, his eyes wide with wonder. "Singing stones," he murmured. "I've heard stories about them, but I never thought I'd see them for myself."

Penelope took a step closer to the circle of stones, her eyes scanning the carvings etched into their surfaces. The symbols were unlike anything she had seen before—twisting lines, spirals, and shapes that seemed to shift slightly as she looked at them. There was something about the arrangement of the stones, something that felt incomplete, as though they were waiting for someone to unlock their full potential.

"What do you think they're singing about?" Penelope wondered aloud.

Jasper twitched his nose, his gaze fixed on the stones. "I'm not sure, but there's definitely something magical going on here. Maybe the stones are trying to tell us something."

Penelope stepped into the circle of stones, her eyes drawn to the largest one at the center. It stood taller than the others, its carvings more elaborate and intricate. As she placed her hand on its cool surface, the melody seemed to shift, the notes rising in intensity, as though the stones were reacting to her presence.

Suddenly, the carvings on the stone beneath her fingers began to glow more brightly, pulsing in time with the music. Penelope felt a surge of energy rush through her, and she knew, without a doubt, that these stones held the key to unlocking the next part of her journey.

"I think they're a puzzle," Penelope said, glancing at Jasper. "If we can figure out how to arrange them correctly, maybe they'll reveal something."

Jasper nodded eagerly. "That makes sense! These stones must be tied to some ancient magic. If we can align them properly, who knows what we might unlock?"

Penelope knelt down in front of the stones, examining them more closely. Each stone had a unique set of carvings, and she could feel a faint hum of energy beneath her fingers as she touched them. The music seemed to guide her, the melody rising and falling in response to her movements, as though the stones were encouraging her to solve their riddle.

"I think we need to move them," Penelope said, standing up and looking around the circle. "But they're too big for me to move on my own."

Jasper scurried over to one of the stones and gave it a push with all his might. "Yeah, no luck on my end either. These things are solid."

Penelope frowned, thinking hard. The stones clearly wanted to be arranged in a specific way, but how could she move them? And then, an idea struck her.

"The music," Penelope said, her eyes lighting up. "It changes when I touch the stones. Maybe it's guiding us."

Jasper nodded, catching on. "Like a clue! If the music gets stronger, we'll know we're on the right track."

Penelope smiled. "Exactly. Let's listen carefully."

With that, Penelope began to move around the circle, touching each stone gently as she listened to the melody. Each time her fingers made contact with the carvings, the music shifted slightly—sometimes growing louder, sometimes softer. It was as though the stones were trying to communicate, guiding her toward the correct arrangement.

After a few minutes, Penelope noticed a pattern. When she touched certain stones in a particular order, the melody grew more harmonious, the notes blending together in perfect unison. She focused on those stones, moving from one to the next, following the music's lead.

"There's a pattern to it," Penelope said, her voice filled with excitement. "We're getting closer."

Jasper watched in awe as Penelope continued to work, her movements deliberate and careful. Finally, after what felt like hours but was likely only minutes, Penelope touched the last stone in the sequence. The moment her fingers made contact, the music swelled to a crescendo, filling the air with a beautiful, haunting melody that seemed to resonate through the entire forest.

The stones began to glow brightly, their carvings pulsing with magic. Slowly, the ground beneath them started to shift, and the largest stone in the center rose higher into the air, revealing a hidden staircase that spiralled downward into the earth.

Penelope and Jasper stared in awe as the hidden entrance was revealed, the music still echoing softly in the background.

"A secret passage," Jasper breathed. "I knew those stones were hiding something!"

Penelope's heart raced with excitement. The stones had unlocked the next part of her adventure, and whatever lay beneath the earth was waiting to be discovered. She took a deep breath, her hand gripping the edge of the staircase.

"We've come this far," Penelope said, glancing at Jasper. "Are you ready?"

Jasper grinned. "You know it."

With that, Penelope and Jasper descended the stone steps, the soft glow of the carvings lighting their way as they ventured deeper into the underground passage. The air grew cooler the further they went, and the music from the stones gradually faded, replaced by the soft drip of water echoing in the distance.

As they reached the bottom of the staircase, Penelope found herself standing in a large, open chamber. The walls were lined with more carvings, similar to those on the stones above, but these were even more detailed, depicting scenes of ancient civilizations, magical creatures, and long-forgotten rituals.

At the center of the chamber stood a stone pedestal, and upon it rested a small, glowing object—an orb that pulsed with a soft, blue light.

"This must be what the stones were guarding," Penelope whispered, her eyes fixed on the orb. "It's beautiful."

Jasper hopped closer to the pedestal, his nose twitching. "Do you think it's another piece of the puzzle? Something that will help us find the Lumen Blossom?"

Penelope nodded. "I think so. The stones wouldn't have led us here unless it was important."

She carefully reached out and picked up the orb, feeling its cool surface pulse gently beneath her fingers. The moment she touched it, a wave of energy rushed through her, and she felt a connection to the magic of the forest—a deep, ancient magic that ran through the land like veins of light.

"We're getting closer," Penelope said softly, a sense of purpose settling over her. "This is part of what we need to save the Butterfly Kingdom."

Jasper nodded, his eyes gleaming with excitement. "Then let's keep going. The Lumen Blossom is out there, and we're one step closer to finding it."

With the orb safely tucked into her satchel and the mystery of the Singing Stones solved, Penelope and Jasper made their way back up the staircase, their hearts filled with determination. The forest still held many secrets, but they were ready for whatever came next.

Chapter 15: The Mischievous Fairies

After retrieving the glowing orb from the Singing Stones, Penelope and Jasper continued their journey through the enchanted forest, their spirits lifted by the progress they had made. The orb pulsed gently from inside Penelope's satchel, its soft blue light a constant reminder of the magic they had uncovered. The next step was clear: they had to find the Lumen Blossom to save the Butterfly Kingdom. But as they walked, the forest around them began to change.

The air grew lighter, and the trees seemed to shimmer with a faint, ethereal glow. Tiny lights flickered in and out of sight, dancing between the branches like stars caught in the breeze. Penelope couldn't help but feel a sense of wonder, as if the forest itself was alive with playful energy.

But Jasper, who had been walking a little ahead, suddenly stopped in his tracks, his ears twitching nervously. "Uh, Penelope? Something doesn't feel right."

Penelope frowned and looked around. At first, she saw nothing out of the ordinary, but then she caught sight of movement—small, darting figures flitting through the air just out of view. She strained her eyes and realized what she was seeing: fairies.

Dozens of them, each no larger than her hand, with delicate wings that shimmered like rainbows. They moved quickly, laughing softly as they zipped from tree to tree, their tiny voices filled with mischief.

"Fairies!" Penelope exclaimed, her eyes widening in surprise. She had read about fairies in stories, but she had never seen them in person before. They were beautiful, but there was something mischievous in the way they moved, something that made Penelope's heart quicken with unease.

Jasper crossed his arms, narrowing his eyes. "Yeah, and they don't look like they're here for a friendly chat."

Before Penelope could respond, one of the fairies darted down from the trees and hovered in front of her face, its tiny wings beating furiously. The fairy had bright blue hair, a mischievous grin, and eyes that sparkled with trouble.

"Well, well, what do we have here?" the fairy said in a high-pitched, sing-song voice. "A human and a squirrel wandering into our territory? How delightful!"

Penelope blinked, taken aback. "We didn't mean to intrude. We're just passing through."

The fairy's grin widened. "Oh, but you're not just passing through. You've entered the realm of the Mischievous Fairies, and we love playing games with newcomers."

Penelope's stomach sank. She had heard stories about fairies and their tricks. They weren't malicious, but they loved to cause confusion, and their games could be unpredictable. She wasn't sure she had time for this—she needed to find the Lumen Blossom.

"Look," Penelope said, trying to keep her voice calm, "we're on an important mission. We're trying to save the Butterfly Kingdom from a dark force. We don't want any trouble."

The fairy giggled, clearly uninterested in Penelope's serious tone. "Oh, we know all about the Butterfly Kingdom and the dark force. But if you want to get through our part of the forest, you'll have to play our games first."

Jasper groaned, his tail flicking in irritation. "Of course we do."

The fairy fluttered higher into the air, signalling to the other fairies. "Come, come! Let's see if this human is as clever as she looks!"

Suddenly, the clearing was filled with fairies. They swarmed around Penelope and Jasper, their laughter echoing through the trees as they flitted about. Penelope felt a pang of anxiety—there were so many of them, and they were clearly eager to cause trouble.

"What kind of games?" Penelope asked, trying to sound braver than she felt.

The blue-haired fairy, who seemed to be the leader, grinned mischievously. "Simple puzzles, of course. If you can outsmart us, we'll let you pass. But if you fail, well..." The fairy's grin widened. "You'll be lost in our forest for a very, very long time."

Penelope's heart raced. She had no choice but to play along. "Alright," she said, squaring her shoulders. "What's the first puzzle?"

The fairies clapped their tiny hands in delight, and one of them, a fairy with bright green wings, zipped forward, holding a small, glowing box in its hands.

"This is a simple one," the green-winged fairy said, its voice bubbling with excitement. "Inside this box is a key, but it's locked tight! To open it, you must figure out the correct sequence of touches on its surface. One wrong move, and the box resets!"

Penelope frowned, examining the glowing box. It had a smooth surface with small, carved symbols—circles, squares, and triangles—arranged in no particular order. The symbols pulsed faintly, and Penelope realized she had to touch them in the right sequence to unlock the box.

"Alright," she muttered to herself. "Let's see..."

She reached out and carefully touched one of the symbols—a triangle. The symbol glowed brightly for a moment, and the box emitted a soft hum. Encouraged, she touched a circle next. This time, the box buzzed, and the glow faded.

Penelope sighed. "Okay, not that combination."

Jasper, who had been watching closely, spoke up. "Try the squares first. They look a bit different from the others."

Penelope nodded and touched one of the squares. The box hummed again, and she quickly followed it with a triangle, then a circle. With a soft click, the box popped open, revealing a small golden key inside.

The fairies cheered, their wings fluttering in excitement. "She solved it! She solved the first puzzle!"

The blue-haired fairy flew down to Penelope, her eyes gleaming with approval. "Well done, human! But don't celebrate too soon. There are more puzzles to solve."

Penelope pocketed the key and took a deep breath. She wasn't out of the woods yet—literally.

The next puzzle was presented by another fairy, this one with bright yellow wings. It held up a small vial of liquid that shimmered in the light.

"This is a special potion," the yellow-winged fairy explained. "It has the power to make something disappear for a short time. But to complete the puzzle, you must figure out which item in this forest will reveal a hidden path when it's gone."

Penelope looked around the clearing, her mind racing. There were trees, bushes, flowers, and rocks all around her, but how could she know which one would reveal the hidden path?

Jasper, who had been pacing nervously, suddenly stopped. "Penelope, remember how the Singing Stones led us to the hidden staircase? Maybe it's the same kind of trick here. Something ordinary could be hiding the path."

Penelope nodded thoughtfully, her eyes scanning the trees. "You're right. But what would be hiding a path?"

She walked slowly around the clearing, examining each object carefully. Finally, her eyes landed on a large tree stump at the edge of the clearing. It looked perfectly ordinary, but something about it seemed off.

"I think it's the stump," Penelope said, her voice steady. "It looks out of place here."

The yellow-winged fairy giggled and handed her the vial. "Let's see if you're right."

Penelope uncorked the vial and poured a few drops of the shimmering liquid onto the stump. Immediately, the stump vanished, revealing a narrow, glowing path that wound through the trees.

The fairies cheered again, their laughter echoing through the forest. "She did it! She found the hidden path!"

The blue-haired fairy fluttered over to Penelope, her mischievous grin softening slightly. "You've outsmarted us twice now. Impressive, human. But we still have one more puzzle for you."

Penelope, feeling more confident now, nodded. "I'm ready. What's the final puzzle?"

The fairy's eyes gleamed as she spoke. "This one is a riddle. Solve it, and you may pass. Fail, and you'll be lost in our forest forever."

Penelope's heart raced, but she nodded, ready to face the challenge.

The blue-haired fairy smiled and recited the riddle in her high, sing-song voice:

"I speak without a mouth and hear without ears.

I have no body, but I come alive with wind.

What am I?"

Penelope frowned, turning the words over in her mind. Speak without a mouth, hear without ears, alive with wind...

Jasper tapped her shoulder. "What do you think it could be?"

Penelope's eyes lit up as the answer clicked in her mind. "It's an echo! It speaks without a mouth and hears without ears, and it needs wind to carry the sound."

The blue-haired fairy's eyes widened in surprise, and then she laughed, a bright, tinkling sound that echoed through the trees. "You're clever, human. Very clever. You've solved all our puzzles!"

The fairies clapped and cheered, and the blue-haired fairy bowed gracefully. "As promised, you may now pass through our forest unharmed. You've earned it."

Penelope smiled, relief washing over her. "Thank you. Your puzzles were challenging, but fun."

The fairies fluttered around her, their wings shimmering in the light as they cleared a path through the forest. "Good luck on your journey, Penelope Pine," the blue-haired fairy said with a grin. "Perhaps we'll meet again, and next time, we'll have even more tricks up our sleeves."

Penelope chuckled. "I'll be ready."

With the fairies' games behind them, Penelope and Jasper continued down the glowing path that had been revealed by the potion. As they left the mischievous fairies behind, Penelope couldn't help but feel a sense of accomplishment. She had outsmarted the tricky creatures and was one step closer to finding the Lumen Blossom.

The adventure was far from over, but with every challenge, Penelope grew stronger, more confident, and more determined to succeed.

Chapter 16: The Sky Pirates

The glowing path left behind by the mischievous fairies led Penelope and Jasper through the forest until they reached the base of a tall, steep hill. The trees here were thinner, their branches swaying in the cool breeze, and as they climbed higher, Penelope noticed the sky shifting from its usual clear blue to a strange, swirling mixture of clouds and mist.

Jasper sniffed the air. "Do you feel that, Penelope? It's different up here. Almost like we're heading into the sky."

Penelope nodded, her heart racing with anticipation. The forest had revealed so many secrets to her already, but something about this place felt otherworldly, as though the air itself was charged with magic.

When they reached the top of the hill, Penelope gasped. Before them, the forest abruptly ended, opening up into a vast, open sky filled with floating islands, each one suspended in mid-air by wisps of clouds. The islands were connected by long, rickety bridges made of wood and rope, swaying gently in the wind. Above them, high in the swirling clouds, Penelope could just make out the faint outlines of ships—ships that sailed not on water, but in the sky.

"Floating islands and sky ships?" Jasper exclaimed, his eyes wide with wonder. "Now this is something I didn't expect."

Penelope's breath caught in her throat. "It's incredible. Look at those ships—they're flying."

As she watched, one of the ships dipped lower, coming into view through the clouds. It was a massive vessel, its wooden hull gleaming in the sunlight. But instead of sails catching the wind, the ship was powered by large propellers and glowing crystals embedded in the hull, which seemed to keep it afloat. On the deck of the ship, Penelope could see figures moving about, adjusting the sails and working the ropes.

Jasper's eyes narrowed. "Those aren't just any travellers. Those are sky pirates."

Before Penelope could respond, the ship began to descend toward them, the sound of its propellers growing louder as it drew near. Penelope and Jasper stepped back, unsure of what to expect.

The ship hovered just above the ground, close enough for Penelope to see the details of its crew. The pirates were a motley bunch, dressed in a mishmash of leathers, scarves, and bandanas, each one adorned with various trinkets and tools. They looked tough, but there was a glint of adventure in their eyes, and Penelope could sense that these pirates were not like the ones she had read about in books. They didn't seem malicious—just wild and free.

A tall figure appeared at the ship's railing and called down to them. "Oi! You two down there! What brings you to the edge of the sky?"

Penelope hesitated, unsure how to answer, but Jasper was quick to speak up. "We're just passing through! What about you? What's a pirate ship doing all the way out here?"

The figure laughed—a hearty, booming sound that echoed through the air. "We're sky pirates, lad! We sail the skies, seeking treasure and adventure wherever the wind takes us."

Penelope stepped forward, feeling a thrill of excitement. "Treasure? What kind of treasure?"

The pirate grinned, his face now clearly visible as the ship hovered lower. He was tall and broad-shouldered, with a patch over one eye and a long coat that fluttered in the wind. "The best kind, lass—the treasure of legends. We're searching for the lost city of Aetheria, hidden somewhere in the clouds."

Penelope's eyes widened. "A lost city in the clouds? Is it real?"

The pirate captain nodded, his expression serious. "Aye, it's real. At least, that's what the old tales say. Aetheria was once a city of scholars and adventurers, a place where magic and knowledge flowed freely. But one day, it vanished—lost to the skies, hidden from all who would seek it. We've been chasing it for years, and we're closer than ever."

Jasper, ever the curious one, leaned forward. "Why are you telling us this? We're just travellers."

The captain's grin returned. "Because you've got the look of adventurers yourselves. We could use a couple of sharp minds on board. What do you say? Care to join the crew of the Stormrider and help us find Aetheria?"

Penelope's heart raced. The idea of joining sky pirates on a floating ship and searching for a lost city was like something out of her wildest dreams. She glanced at Jasper, who seemed equally excited.

"Well," Penelope said, smiling, "we are on a quest of our own. We're searching for the Lumen Blossom to save the Butterfly Kingdom. But if helping you brings us closer to our goal, we'd be happy to join you."

The captain laughed again. "Then welcome aboard, lass! The Stormrider is always open to adventurers with a good cause. The Lumen Blossom, you say? A rare and powerful flower, indeed. Who knows? Perhaps our paths to treasure and your quest for the blossom are one and the same."

Without further hesitation, the crew lowered a rope ladder, and Penelope and Jasper climbed aboard the Stormrider. As soon as they were safely on deck, the ship rose higher into the sky, leaving the ground far below. Penelope's heart soared with excitement as she looked out over the horizon, the floating islands drifting lazily in the distance.

The captain strode over to them, clapping Penelope on the back. "I'm Captain Marlowe, by the way. And this is my crew—the finest sky pirates you'll ever meet."

The crew cheered and waved at Penelope and Jasper, their faces filled with a mixture of curiosity and camaraderie. One pirate, a young woman with a headscarf and a belt filled with tools, stepped forward and grinned. "Welcome to the skies, newcomers! I'm Tessa, the ship's mechanic. I keep the Stormrider in tip-top shape."

Another pirate, a lean man with a bright red coat and a pair of brass goggles perched on his head, tipped his hat. "And I'm Quinn. Navigator, map-maker, and occasional prankster."

Penelope smiled at them all. She had never felt more at home in such a strange place. "It's nice to meet all of you. We're looking forward to helping with your search."

Captain Marlowe led them to the ship's helm, where a large, ancient map was spread out across a wooden table. The map was filled with strange symbols, cloud formations, and marks that indicated various floating islands.

"We believe Aetheria lies somewhere near the Skyveil, a thick cloud formation that's nearly impossible to navigate," Captain Marlowe explained, pointing to a swirling mass of clouds on the map. "But we've found clues—ancient runes and hidden texts—that suggest a path through the veil. We'll need sharp eyes and quick thinking to find the way."

Penelope studied the map, feeling the weight of the adventure ahead. "What kind of clues have you found?"

Quinn grinned, pulling out a small, glowing compass. "We found this a few weeks ago. It's said to point the way to Aetheria, but the trick is, it doesn't just point north. It reacts to magic—specifically, to ancient magic like the kind that kept Aetheria hidden."

Penelope's eyes lit up. "That sounds a lot like the magic we've been encountering in the forest—the Singing Stones, the enchanted map…"

Tessa nodded thoughtfully. "That's exactly what we've been thinking. The magic in this part of the world is all connected, and Aetheria is at the heart of it. If you've been following ancient magic, you're on the right path."

Jasper twitched his tail, clearly excited. "So, what's next? How do we find the path through the Skyveil?"

Captain Marlowe rubbed his chin, his eyes gleaming with anticipation. "We follow the compass and the clues we've gathered.

But there's one more thing we'll need—a Sky Shard, a piece of ancient crystal said to help navigate the most dangerous parts of the veil. We've heard rumours of one hidden on a nearby island."

Penelope nodded, her heart pounding. "Then let's go find it."

With the wind at their backs and the vast sky stretching out before them, the Stormrider set sail for the floating island where the Sky Shard was said to be hidden. Penelope and Jasper stood at the railing, watching the clouds drift by, feeling the thrill of adventure surge through them.

The journey was far from over, and the search for the Lumen Blossom still lay ahead. But with the sky pirates by their side, Penelope knew they were one step closer to uncovering the lost secrets of the forest—and perhaps even the fabled city of Aetheria.

Chapter 17: The Shapeshifter's Secret

The Stormrider sailed smoothly through the skies, the crew working diligently as the ship drifted between floating islands and shimmering clouds. Penelope and Jasper had settled into life with the sky pirates, helping with small tasks and learning more about the mysterious lost city of Aetheria. Yet, as the ship ventured deeper into the swirling skies near the Skyveil, Penelope couldn't shake the feeling that something—or someone—was watching them.

The sky was growing darker, the clouds thick and heavy as they neared their destination. The island where the Sky Shard was hidden loomed ahead, a jagged mass of rock and dense foliage floating in the mist. It seemed wild and untouched, with cliffs that dropped into the endless sky below.

Captain Marlowe, standing at the helm, squinted at the horizon. "We're getting close. Keep your eyes sharp—this island's been known to have some strange inhabitants."

Tessa, the ship's mechanic, nodded. "There've been tales of creatures who can change their form, blending in with the island. Best we stay cautious."

Penelope's curiosity flared. Shapeshifters? She had read about them in fairy tales, but never thought she would encounter one. Still, there was a part of her that was excited—what if this shapeshifter could help her find the Sky Shard or give her a clue to the Lumen Blossom?

As the Stormrider touched down on the island's rocky surface, the crew lowered the gangplank, and Penelope, Jasper, and a few pirates disembarked. The island was eerily quiet, the wind whispering through the trees and the faint sound of birds calling from the distance.

Jasper sniffed the air, his ears twitching nervously. "I don't like this place. It feels...off."

Penelope nodded, feeling the tension in the air. "Let's stick together and keep an eye out for anything unusual."

The group ventured further into the island's dense jungle, following a narrow path that wound through the trees. The air was thick with the scent of moss and damp earth, and every rustle of leaves made Penelope's heart race. She kept her hand on the enchanted map in her satchel, ready to use it if necessary.

Suddenly, the jungle opened up into a clearing, and standing in the middle of it was a figure—a tall, graceful figure cloaked in shadows. Penelope froze, her eyes widening as she realized what she was seeing.

The figure shifted and changed before her eyes, its form melting from that of a tall, shadowy person into that of a sleek, black panther. The panther's yellow eyes gleamed in the fading light, and then, with another swift movement, it transformed again—this time into a young woman with silver hair and piercing green eyes.

"A shapeshifter," Jasper whispered, his voice barely audible.

The woman smiled, her gaze fixed on Penelope. "You're not like the others," she said, her voice smooth and melodic. "You're searching for something, aren't you?"

Penelope swallowed hard, trying to stay calm. "Yes, we're looking for the Sky Shard. Do you know where it is?"

The shapeshifter's smile widened, but there was something unsettling in her expression—something secretive. "The Sky Shard is here, on this island. But why should I help you find it?"

Jasper, ever cautious, crossed his arms. "What do you want in return?"

The shapeshifter tilted her head, her green eyes gleaming with mischief. "Ah, you're clever. Yes, there is something I want. You see, I've been on this island for many years, trapped by the magic of the clouds. I can take any form I please, but I cannot leave. If you help me break my curse, I will give you the Sky Shard."

Penelope frowned. Something about the shapeshifter's offer didn't sit right with her. Why was she cursed? And if she was freed, what kind of danger would she pose? The shapeshifter's motives were unclear, and

Penelope didn't trust her fully. But she also knew they needed the Sky Shard to continue their quest.

"How do we know you're telling the truth?" Penelope asked carefully.

The shapeshifter's smile faltered for a moment, her eyes narrowing slightly. "You don't. But I'm your only chance of finding the Sky Shard. Without me, you'll never reach it."

Penelope exchanged a glance with Jasper. The shapeshifter was cunning, that much was clear. But Penelope had dealt with tricky characters before, and she knew she needed to be smart about this.

"All right," Penelope said slowly. "We'll help you break the curse, but first, we need to see the Sky Shard."

The shapeshifter's eyes gleamed with amusement. "A bold move. Very well. Follow me."

With a fluid motion, the shapeshifter transformed into a hawk and took off into the sky, soaring high above the trees. Penelope and Jasper hurried after her, following the direction of her flight as she led them deeper into the island's interior. After a short while, they reached a hidden grove, where a large stone altar stood at the center.

Hovering above the altar was the Sky Shard.

The shard was a crystalline fragment, glowing with a soft, blue light. It pulsed with ancient magic, its surface shimmering with the power of the skies. Penelope's heart raced as she approached it—this was what they had been searching for.

The shapeshifter, now back in her human form, stood beside the altar, watching Penelope closely. "There it is—the Sky Shard, as promised. But you will not touch it until my curse is broken."

Penelope studied the shapeshifter carefully. "How do we break the curse?"

The shapeshifter's expression darkened. "There is a stone, hidden deep within the caves beneath this island. It is the source of the curse that binds me here. Destroy the stone, and I will be free."

Jasper narrowed his eyes, his voice low. "And what happens once you're free? What will you do?"

The shapeshifter smiled, but there was no warmth in it. "I will do what all creatures of the sky do—I will be free to roam where I please."

Penelope's mind raced. The shapeshifter had been trapped on the island for years, and while her offer seemed genuine, Penelope couldn't help but feel that there was more to her story. If they freed her, would she become an ally—or a threat?

"Why were you cursed in the first place?" Penelope asked, her voice firm.

The shapeshifter's eyes flashed with irritation. "That is none of your concern. Do you want the Sky Shard or not?"

Penelope's suspicions deepened. The shapeshifter was hiding something—something important. But without the Sky Shard, their quest to save the Butterfly Kingdom would be at a standstill.

Penelope took a deep breath and made her decision. "We'll help you, but we want a promise. If we break your curse, you won't harm anyone. You'll leave this island in peace."

The shapeshifter's smile returned, sly and calculating. "I am a creature of my word. Free me, and I will cause no harm to you or your friends."

Penelope nodded, though doubt still lingered in her heart. She had made her choice, but she knew she had to remain cautious. The shapeshifter was powerful, and there was no telling what she would do once freed.

With a final glance at the Sky Shard, Penelope and Jasper followed the shapeshifter's directions, making their way toward the caves beneath the island. The path was steep and treacherous, but they pressed on, their determination fuelled by the knowledge that they were one step closer to completing their quest.

As they entered the dark, winding cave, Penelope couldn't shake the feeling that they were walking into a trap. The shapeshifter's true motives were still unclear, and Penelope knew she had to be ready for anything.

The stone that held the shapeshifter's curse lay somewhere within these caves—and Penelope was about to discover the secret that had bound the mysterious creature to the island for so many years.

Chapter 18: The Wild Chase

The dark, twisting cave beneath the island felt like it stretched on forever. Penelope and Jasper made their way through the narrow passages, guided only by the faint light of the enchanted map and the steady pulse of the Sky Shard's magic in the distance. Every step felt like it brought them deeper into the unknown, and Penelope's nerves were on edge, especially after the strange encounter with the shapeshifter.

"This place gives me the creeps," Jasper muttered, his voice echoing slightly off the stone walls. "I don't trust that shapeshifter. There's something she's not telling us."

Penelope nodded, her mind still racing with doubts. "I know. We need to be careful. I don't think she told us the whole truth about her curse."

As they descended further into the cave, the air grew colder, and an eerie silence settled around them. The only sound was their footsteps and the occasional drip of water from the cave ceiling. Penelope couldn't shake the feeling that something was watching them—lurking in the shadows, waiting for the right moment to strike.

Suddenly, a distant rumble echoed through the cave, followed by a strange, guttural growl that made Penelope's blood run cold.

"What was that?" Jasper whispered, his eyes wide with alarm.

Penelope's heart pounded in her chest. "I don't know, but it's getting closer."

The growl echoed again, this time louder, and Penelope felt a shiver run down her spine. Whatever it was, it was coming for them—and fast.

"Run!" Penelope shouted, grabbing Jasper and sprinting down the narrow passageway.

They raced through the cave, their footsteps echoing as the mysterious creature behind them roared again, the sound bouncing off the stone walls. Penelope could feel the vibrations of its heavy footsteps getting closer, and panic surged through her veins. She had no idea what was chasing them, but she knew it was dangerous.

The passageway twisted and turned, and Penelope's heart raced as she struggled to find a way out. The enchanted map pulsed in her hand, but the cave's labyrinthine passages were too complex to navigate in the heat of the moment. She needed a plan—and fast.

As they rounded a corner, Penelope skidded to a halt, her eyes landing on a narrow crevice in the rock wall. It was barely wide enough for them to squeeze through, but it might offer them a temporary hiding place.

"In here!" Penelope whispered urgently, tugging Jasper toward the crevice.

They scrambled into the narrow opening, pressing themselves flat against the cool stone. Penelope held her breath, her heart pounding in her ears as the sound of heavy footsteps grew louder. Whatever was chasing them was close—too close.

For a moment, the creature's growls filled the air, and Penelope felt a wave of dread wash over her. She dared not look around the corner, but she could sense the creature lurking just beyond their hiding place. The air was thick with tension, and she could almost hear the creature's breath as it sniffed the air, searching for them.

Then, without warning, the sound of footsteps moved away, and the creature's growls faded into the distance.

Penelope let out a shaky breath, relief flooding through her. Jasper, still pressed against her shoulder, whispered, "That was too close."

Penelope nodded, wiping the sweat from her brow. "I don't think we've lost it for good. We need to keep moving."

They cautiously emerged from the crevice and continued deeper into the cave, moving quickly but quietly. The map glowed faintly in Penelope's hand, but its lines were becoming more erratic, the magic reacting to the presence of whatever was hunting them. The creature was still nearby, and it seemed to be closing in on them.

As they moved, Penelope noticed something strange about the cave walls. The carvings etched into the stone—similar to the ones they had seen near the Sky Shard—began to glow faintly, pulsing in time with the map's magic. It was as if the cave itself was alive with ancient energy, guiding them toward something.

Penelope's mind raced. The carvings—perhaps they were clues. The enchanted map had always shown her the way before, but maybe now it was the cave that held the answers. She ran her fingers along the glowing symbols, trying to decipher their meaning.

Suddenly, the ground beneath them trembled, and the guttural growl of the creature echoed through the cave again, closer this time. Penelope's heart skipped a beat as she realized the creature was catching up.

"We need to figure this out, fast," she muttered, her eyes scanning the carvings.

Jasper, ever the quick thinker, pointed to a section of the wall where the carvings formed a circular pattern. "Look! That symbol—it's the same as the one on the map!"

Penelope's eyes lit up. "You're right! Maybe it's a way out."

Without hesitation, Penelope pressed her hand against the circular carving. The stone wall shuddered, and slowly, a hidden door slid open, revealing a narrow tunnel leading deeper into the cave.

"This has to be the way," Penelope said, pulling Jasper through the door.

As soon as they stepped into the tunnel, the door slid shut behind them, sealing them off from the main passage. The growls of the creature echoed faintly on the other side, but for now, they were safe.

Penelope leaned against the wall, catching her breath. "That was close."

Jasper, still shaking slightly, gave a nervous laugh. "Too close. Whatever's chasing us isn't giving up easily."

Penelope nodded, her mind racing. "We have to stay ahead of it. This tunnel seems different—it's like the magic here is stronger. Maybe it'll lead us to the stone we're supposed to destroy."

They continued down the tunnel, the glowing carvings guiding their way. The air felt charged with energy, and Penelope could sense that they were getting closer to something important.

After what felt like an eternity, the tunnel opened up into a large chamber. At the center of the chamber stood a massive stone, its surface covered in ancient runes that glowed with dark energy. Penelope's heart pounded as she realized this was the stone that held the shapeshifter's curse.

But as they approached the stone, a deafening roar echoed through the chamber, and Penelope's blood ran cold. The creature was here.

Bursting into the chamber, the creature finally revealed itself. It was a hulking, monstrous thing—part shadow, part flesh, with glowing red eyes and long, jagged claws that scraped the stone floor. Its body seemed to ripple and shift, as if it were made of darkness itself.

Penelope's mind raced. She had to destroy the stone—but how? The creature was blocking their path, and there was no time to think.

Suddenly, the enchanted map pulsed in her hand, and Penelope glanced down at it. The glowing lines on the map had shifted, revealing a single path—a line of energy leading from the map to the stone.

"The map," Penelope whispered. "It's showing us what to do."

With a surge of determination, Penelope ran toward the stone, her heart pounding in her chest. She could hear the creature's growls behind her, but she didn't look back. She focused on the map's magic, following its guidance.

As she reached the stone, Penelope placed her hand on its surface, and the runes began to glow brighter, pulsing with dark energy. But the map's magic surged through her, and with a burst of light, the runes cracked and shattered.

The stone crumbled to the ground, its magic dissolving into the air. The creature let out a final, furious roar before it, too, dissolved into shadows, vanishing from the chamber.

Penelope collapsed to her knees, breathing heavily. The curse was broken. The creature was gone.

Jasper rushed to her side, his eyes wide with relief. "You did it, Penelope. You destroyed the stone."

Penelope nodded, her heart still racing. "And now, the shapeshifter is free."

With the curse broken and the creature defeated, Penelope and Jasper made their way back through the cave, their path now clear. The shapeshifter's secret had been uncovered, and their journey toward the Sky Shard—and the Lumen Blossom—continued.

Chapter 19: The Frozen Kingdom

After their narrow escape from the cave and the defeat of the mysterious creature, Penelope and Jasper returned to the Stormrider with the knowledge that the shapeshifter's curse had been broken. The Sky Shard now lay safely in Penelope's satchel, it's cool glow a constant reminder of the power it held. But their journey wasn't over yet. The Skyveil still loomed ahead, and somewhere beyond it, the Lumen Blossom waited.

As the ship sailed farther into the misty skies, the air grew colder, and the clouds took on a strange, shimmering quality. Penelope stood at the railing, staring out at the swirling white expanse ahead. There was something different about this place—something ancient and still. Even the crew of the Stormrider had grown quiet, as if they sensed the approaching mystery.

Jasper, perched on Penelope's shoulder, rubbed his paws together to keep warm. "I've got a bad feeling about this. It's freezing up here."

Penelope nodded, pulling her cloak tighter around her shoulders. "We're close to something. I can feel it."

Suddenly, a flicker of movement in the clouds caught Penelope's eye. As she squinted into the distance, she saw it—a towering structure of ice, half-hidden by the swirling mist. It was a massive castle, its spires and turrets glittering like crystal, but there was something eerie about it. The castle seemed...silent, as though frozen in time.

"Look," Penelope whispered, pointing toward the castle. "There's something down there."

Captain Marlowe joined her at the railing, his one good eye scanning the horizon. "That's no ordinary place. A kingdom made of ice? We're in uncharted territory now."

As the Stormrider descended toward the icy castle, Penelope noticed more details. Surrounding the castle were buildings—an entire village, frozen solid, with streets, homes, and gardens all covered in layers of snow and ice. But what struck her most was the stillness. There were people here—figures standing in the streets, at their doorways, and in the gardens—but they were frozen, locked in place as though time itself had stopped.

The ship touched down just outside the castle walls, and Penelope and Jasper disembarked with Captain Marlowe and a few of the crew. The moment her feet touched the icy ground, a chill ran through Penelope's bones. It wasn't just the cold—it was the feeling that this place had been trapped, abandoned to winter's grip for centuries.

"This place..." Penelope whispered, looking around. "It's frozen in time."

Jasper hopped off her shoulder, his tiny paws sinking into the snow. "Look at the people—they're not just frozen. It's like they're in the middle of living their lives, but something stopped them."

Penelope walked through the snow-covered streets, passing by the frozen inhabitants. There was a woman holding a basket of fruit, a child reaching up to grab something from a high shelf, and a man halfway through closing the door to his home. Their faces were peaceful, as if they had no idea what had happened. It was as though they had been frozen in a single moment—caught between one heartbeat and the next.

"What could have done this?" Penelope wondered aloud, her voice echoing in the stillness.

Captain Marlowe shook his head, his expression grim. "Whatever magic this is, it's powerful. There's no telling how long these people have been trapped."

Jasper shivered, looking around warily. "We've got to do something to help them, but how do you thaw an entire kingdom?"

Penelope's mind raced as she tried to piece together what had happened. The enchanted map glowed faintly in her hand, but it offered no clear solution. She glanced up at the towering ice castle ahead and felt a pull toward it. If there were answers, they would be in there.

"We need to get inside the castle," Penelope said, determination filling her voice. "Whatever caused this—it's in there."

Captain Marlowe nodded. "We'll follow your lead, lass. But be on your guard. If there's magic strong enough to freeze an entire kingdom, we don't know what else might be lurking in that castle."

With that, Penelope, Jasper, and the crew made their way toward the castle gates. The entrance was blocked by massive doors of solid ice, but with some effort, they managed to pry them open, revealing a grand hall beyond. The interior of the castle was just as cold and still as the village outside. Icicles hung from the ceilings, and the floor was slick with frost. The frozen inhabitants of the castle stood motionless in the hall, their regal clothes coated in shimmering frost.

At the far end of the hall, seated upon a grand ice throne, was a figure that caught Penelope's attention. It was a woman, her skin pale as snow, her long hair trailing down her back like strands of frost. She was dressed in a gown of ice, and her hands were raised as though she had been about to cast a spell. But like the others, she was frozen—caught in time, locked in her final moment.

"That must be the queen," Penelope whispered, approaching the throne. "She was the one who ruled this kingdom."

Jasper looked up at the frozen queen, his ears twitching nervously. "Do you think she's the one who caused this?"

Penelope frowned, studying the queen's peaceful expression. "Maybe...or maybe she was trying to stop it."

As she drew closer to the throne, Penelope noticed something strange at the queen's feet—a small, glowing object half-buried in the ice. She knelt down and brushed away the frost, revealing a shimmering crystal, similar to the one that powered the Sky Shard but colder, its surface radiating icy magic.

"This must be the source of the freezing magic," Penelope said, holding up the crystal. "But it feels like it's not working properly—it's unstable."

Captain Marlowe approached, his brow furrowed. "Can you fix it? If this crystal is what's holding the kingdom in eternal winter, maybe you can use it to reverse the spell."

Penelope studied the crystal closely, feeling the pulse of its magic. It was powerful, but it was fractured, its energy leaking out in unpredictable ways. She realized that the crystal hadn't meant to freeze the kingdom—it had malfunctioned, and its magic had spread out of control, trapping everything in a never-ending winter.

"I think I can fix it," Penelope said, her voice steady. "But I'll need help. We have to channel the magic in the right way, or it could make things worse."

Jasper hopped onto her shoulder. "We're with you, Penelope. Tell us what to do."

Penelope took a deep breath and placed the crystal on the ground in front of her. "We need to focus on warmth—on the idea of thawing the kingdom, not just breaking the spell. If we disrupt the magic too suddenly, it could destroy everything."

Captain Marlowe nodded. "We'll follow your lead."

Penelope closed her eyes and placed her hands on the crystal, feeling its cold energy pulsing through her. She focused on warmth, on the memory of summer days, on the feeling of the sun on her skin. Slowly, she channelled that energy into the crystal, guiding the fractured magic back into balance.

The crystal began to glow brighter, its icy light warming to a soft, golden hue. Penelope could feel the magic shifting, pulling away from the frozen kingdom and retreating back into the crystal.

Suddenly, a crack echoed through the grand hall, and the ice around the queen's throne began to melt. Penelope opened her eyes to see the frost receding, the frozen inhabitants beginning to thaw. The queen's hands lowered, and her eyes fluttered open as if she were waking from a long sleep.

Penelope's heart raced. It was working.

The ice continued to melt, the warmth spreading through the castle and out into the village beyond. The frozen people blinked and looked around in confusion, as though no time had passed at all.

The queen slowly stood from her throne, her pale blue eyes filled with wonder. She looked down at Penelope, who still held the glowing crystal, and smiled.

"You..." the queen whispered, her voice soft but powerful. "You saved us."

Penelope smiled, relief washing over her. "The crystal—it wasn't working properly. I was able to fix it."

The queen nodded, her gaze drifting to the thawing kingdom outside. "We have been frozen in time for centuries. I tried to stop the spell, but the magic was too strong. You have restored us."

Jasper grinned, his tail flicking with excitement. "So that means the kingdom is free now, right?"

The queen smiled warmly. "Yes, we are free. Thanks to you."

As the last of the ice melted away and the kingdom began to awaken, Penelope stood tall, the crystal glowing softly in her hands. The kingdom of eternal winter had been thawed, and its people were free once more.

With the curse lifted, Penelope and Jasper returned to the Stormrider, ready to continue their journey. The Lumen Blossom was still waiting to be found, but now, with the frozen kingdom restored, they were one step closer to completing their quest.

Chapter 20: The Magic Compass

The sky above the Stormrider cleared as Penelope, Jasper, and the crew sailed away from the recently thawed Frozen Kingdom. The weight of the kingdom's curse was gone, replaced by the warmth of the sun and a renewed sense of hope. Penelope, her heart light, felt as though they were finally on the right path. Still, the mystery of the Lumen Blossom and the dangerous Skyveil lay ahead, waiting to be unravelled.

After their long day of adventure, Penelope sat on the deck of the ship, gazing out over the horizon. She absentmindedly ran her fingers along the enchanted map, which had led her this far. The map had been a faithful guide, but something tugged at her mind—there were still mysteries in the forest and sky that the map couldn't predict.

Suddenly, Captain Marlowe approached, holding a small, ornate box. "Penelope, lass," he said, his gruff voice softening as he spoke, "I think it's time I gave you something. This may help you on your journey."

Penelope looked up, curious. "What is it?"

The captain smiled slightly and handed her the box. "It's an old pirate treasure, but it's not gold or jewels. This is a magic compass—an artifact that's been in our crew for as long as I can remember. It doesn't just point north like an ordinary compass. No, this one points to wherever you need to go next... whatever adventure awaits."

Penelope's eyes widened with excitement. "A magic compass?"

Captain Marlowe nodded. "Aye, but it comes with a warning. This compass not only shows you the way to your next adventure, but it also warns you of the dangers that lie ahead. When it glows red, there's trouble on the horizon."

Penelope carefully opened the small box and gasped. Inside was a beautifully crafted brass compass, its surface etched with swirling patterns and symbols. The compass needle was unlike any she had ever seen—it didn't point north, but instead spun slowly, as though waiting for her to decide her next move.

"Thank you," Penelope said, her voice filled with awe. "This will be a huge help on our journey."

Captain Marlowe grinned. "It's served us well over the years, and I have a feeling it'll do the same for you. Trust it, but remember—heed its warnings."

Penelope nodded as she held the compass in her hands, feeling the cool metal beneath her fingertips. The enchanted map had been invaluable, but this compass would give her something more—an intuition about the path ahead. It would guide her, not just with landmarks and destinations, but with a deeper sense of where her next challenge lay.

As she stood there, the needle of the compass began to spin faster, the magic within it stirring. After a moment, the needle pointed straight ahead, toward a distant part of the sky. Penelope felt a strange pull, as though the compass itself was urging her forward.

Jasper, who had been watching the whole exchange from atop a barrel, hopped down and peered over Penelope's shoulder. "Where's it pointing now?"

Penelope followed the needle's direction, her eyes narrowing at the sky ahead. "It's leading us somewhere... but I can't tell where. I think it's our next destination."

Jasper's tail flicked with excitement. "Well, what are we waiting for? Let's follow it!"

Captain Marlowe, overhearing them, called out to the crew. "You heard the girl! Set course for the direction of the magic compass!"

The crew of the Stormrider sprang into action, adjusting the sails and steering the ship toward the unknown. The sky ahead was clear, but there was a tension in the air, as if something unseen waited just beyond the horizon. Penelope glanced down at the compass again. The needle glowed faintly, but the red warning light remained dormant—for now.

As the ship sailed onward, Penelope and Jasper stood at the bow, the wind whipping through their hair. The magic compass remained steady, guiding them forward, but Penelope couldn't shake the feeling that something was approaching—something important, yet dangerous.

Hours passed, and the sky began to darken. The once-clear air was now filled with ominous clouds, and the temperature dropped sharply. Penelope's hand tightened around the compass as she saw the needle quiver, its glow turning from soft white to an unsettling red.

Jasper noticed the change immediately. "Uh-oh. It's warning us about something, isn't it?"

Penelope nodded, her heart quickening. "Something's coming. We need to be ready."

Before she could say anything else, a low rumble echoed through the air, and the clouds ahead began to swirl violently. A massive storm was brewing, its winds howling through the sky, and in the distance, Penelope could make out the shadow of something large moving through the storm.

"What is that?" she whispered, her eyes wide.

The crew scrambled to secure the sails as Captain Marlowe shouted commands, his voice barely audible over the rising wind. "Brace yourselves, everyone! We've sailed into a storm, and there's something big out there!"

Penelope's heart raced as she clutched the compass. The needle pointed directly toward the storm, glowing an ominous red. Whatever was lurking in those clouds, it was their next challenge—and it wasn't friendly.

Suddenly, a massive shape emerged from the swirling clouds. It was a creature—enormous, with wings that stretched across the sky and glowing eyes that pierced through the storm. Its body was made of dark, crackling energy, as if the storm itself had taken form and come to life.

"A storm beast!" Captain Marlowe shouted. "We've encountered them before, but this one is the largest I've seen!"

The creature roared, its voice like thunder, and it dove toward the Stormrider, its massive wings flapping with the force of a gale. The ship rocked violently as the storm beast's winds slammed into it, and Penelope and Jasper struggled to keep their footing.

"Penelope!" Jasper shouted over the roar of the storm. "What do we do?"

Penelope's mind raced. The compass had led them here, but why? There had to be a reason—a clue or a way to defeat the storm beast. She glanced down at the magic compass, watching the needle spin wildly in response to the danger. Then, suddenly, it stopped, pointing directly to the left of the ship.

"The compass is showing us something," Penelope said urgently. "We need to head in that direction!"

Captain Marlowe nodded, steering the Stormrider as best he could toward the compass's direction. The storm beast roared again, its claws swiping at the ship, but the crew managed to hold steady, the ship dodging the worst of the creature's attacks.

As they sailed toward the compass's target, Penelope spotted something through the thick clouds—an island, hidden in the eye of the storm. It was small but glowing with a strange, golden light, as if it held the answer they were seeking.

"That island!" Penelope shouted. "We have to get to it!"

The crew steered the ship toward the island, dodging the storm beast's attacks as best they could. The magic compass's glow grew stronger, guiding them through the chaos. Penelope's heart raced as they neared the island, the storm closing in around them.

Finally, with a final burst of speed, the Stormrider reached the island's shore. The moment they touched down, the storm beast let out an ear-splitting roar and disappeared into the clouds, its form dissolving like mist.

The storm began to calm, the winds dying down as the golden glow of the island surrounded them. Penelope and Jasper disembarked, their eyes wide with wonder as they stepped onto the sandy shore.

In the center of the island stood a pedestal, and atop it was a small, glowing crystal—similar to the Sky Shard, but pulsing with warm, golden energy.

"This must be what the compass was leading us to," Penelope whispered, approaching the pedestal. "Another shard of ancient magic."

Jasper nodded. "It must be. But what does it do?"

Penelope carefully picked up the crystal, feeling its warmth spread through her fingers. The moment she touched it, the magic compass glowed brightly, the red warning light fading away.

"The compass led us here to protect us," Penelope said, her voice filled with awe. "This crystal—it has the power to calm the storm. That's why the storm beast left."

With the crystal in hand, Penelope and Jasper returned to the Stormrider, the island's golden light still glowing softly behind them. The storm had cleared, and the sky was calm once more. As the ship sailed away, Penelope felt a surge of hope. The magic compass had not only guided them to their next adventure but had also saved them from the dangers ahead.

Their journey continued, and Penelope knew that with the compass by her side, she would always be one step ahead of whatever dangers lay on the horizon.

Chapter 21: The Crystal Cavern

After the storm cleared and the Stormrider sailed safely through the skies, Penelope's thoughts turned to the next part of her journey. The magic compass, now an essential tool in her quest, had proven its value, guiding her through dangers and leading her to safety. But its needle continued to spin, pointing toward an unknown destination, its faint glow urging her forward. Whatever the next adventure held, Penelope knew it would reveal something important.

As they sailed, the clouds parted, and far below, Penelope spotted a landscape of jagged mountains and valleys, their rocky surfaces glimmering with an eerie, bluish light. The magic compass pointed steadily in their direction, and Penelope felt a strange pull, as though something was waiting for her among those glowing peaks.

Captain Marlowe joined her at the railing, his one good eye scanning the horizon. "Looks like we're headed toward the Crystal Cavern," he said, his voice low. "It's a place of ancient magic, hidden deep within the mountains. But be warned, lass—it's said that the crystals inside show you more than just your reflection. They reveal things... things about your future."

Penelope's heart skipped a beat. "A place that shows you the future?"

Marlowe nodded. "Aye, but not all futures are bright. The Crystal Cavern doesn't show you what will happen—only what could happen. The choices you make, the paths you walk—they all lead to different possibilities. The cavern shows them all."

Jasper, perched on Penelope's shoulder, raised an eyebrow. "Sounds risky. But knowing Penelope, I'm guessing she's already decided to go."

Penelope smiled slightly, her curiosity getting the better of her. "I have to see it. If the crystals can help me understand what's coming, then I need to go. It might even help us find the Lumen Blossom."

With the captain's approval, the crew lowered the Stormrider toward the mountain range. As the ship neared the ground, Penelope could see the faint glow of the cavern's entrance—an archway of jagged rocks surrounded by glowing blue crystals. The air was cool and crisp, filled with the hum of energy that seemed to pulse from the stones themselves.

Penelope and Jasper disembarked, their footsteps crunching on the rocky path as they made their way toward the cavern. The closer they got, the brighter the crystals became, casting an otherworldly glow across the landscape. The entrance to the cavern loomed ahead, dark and mysterious, the glow from the crystals drawing them inside like a beacon.

"Here we go," Penelope said softly, taking a deep breath. She glanced at Jasper. "Are you ready?"

Jasper gave her a nervous grin. "As ready as I'll ever be. Let's see what these crystals have to say."

Together, they stepped into the Crystal Cavern.

The moment they entered, Penelope felt the air change. It was thick with magic, and the walls of the cavern glittered with thousands of crystals, each one reflecting a different light. The crystals pulsed softly, casting long shadows on the floor and ceiling, and the deeper they went, the more mesmerizing the glow became. It was as if the entire cavern was alive, humming with ancient energy.

Jasper's eyes darted around. "This place... it's beautiful, but kind of eerie, too."

Penelope nodded, her breath catching in her throat as they ventured deeper into the cavern. The walls around them were covered in crystals of every shape and size, each one glowing with a unique color—some soft and warm, others cold and sharp. As Penelope looked closer, she noticed something strange. Each crystal seemed to shimmer not just with light, but with images—fleeting glimpses of scenes, moments in time, that flickered in and out of view.

"These crystals..." Penelope whispered, stepping closer to one of the larger formations. "They're showing me something."

She reached out to touch the crystal, and the moment her fingers brushed its surface, the image inside became clearer. It was a scene—Penelope standing in a forest clearing, holding the Lumen Blossom in her hands. The glow of the magical flower illuminated her face, and she smiled, victorious.

Jasper leaned over to look at the crystal. "Is that... the future?"

Penelope nodded, her heart racing. "It's one possible future. A future where we find the Lumen Blossom."

She moved to another crystal, her curiosity driving her forward. This time, the image inside the crystal was different. It showed Penelope in the middle of a storm, her face pale and worried as dark clouds swirled around her. The Stormrider was nowhere to be seen, and she stood alone, facing an unseen danger.

Penelope pulled her hand back, a chill running down her spine. "This one... it shows me lost, separated from everyone."

Jasper frowned. "So, each crystal shows a different version of what could happen. But how do we know which future is the one that'll come true?"

Penelope bit her lip. "We don't. The future is always changing, based on the choices we make."

They continued deeper into the cavern, passing by more crystals, each one showing different possibilities. Some showed Penelope victorious, finding the Lumen Blossom and saving the Butterfly Kingdom. Others showed her trapped, lost, or facing dangers far greater than she had imagined. There were futures where she stood alone, and others where she was surrounded by friends and allies.

As Penelope studied the different futures, she felt a sense of unease growing inside her. It was overwhelming, seeing all the possibilities laid out before her. Every choice she made, every step she took, could lead to a different outcome. The pressure to make the right decision weighed heavily on her shoulders.

Suddenly, Penelope's attention was drawn to a large, central crystal, taller than the rest. Its surface was smooth, and unlike the others, it didn't show fragmented images or fleeting glimpses. Instead, the crystal glowed steadily, its light pulsing with a calm, steady rhythm.

Penelope approached it cautiously. "This one feels... different."

Jasper peered at the crystal. "It's not showing anything. Do you think it's broken?"

Penelope shook her head. "No. I think this crystal shows something deeper."

She placed her hand on the crystal, and the moment her skin touched its surface, the cavern around her faded away. Suddenly, Penelope was standing in the middle of a forest clearing—one she had never seen before. The air was thick with magic, and in the center of the clearing, growing out of the ground like a beacon of light, was the Lumen Blossom.

Penelope's breath caught in her throat. "This is it. This is where we need to go."

The vision shifted, and Penelope saw herself standing beside Jasper, the Lumen Blossom in her hands. But there was something else in the vision—a shadow, lurking at the edge of the clearing, watching her. It was tall, with glowing eyes, its presence sending a wave of fear through Penelope's heart. The shadow seemed to pulse with dark energy, as though it was waiting for the right moment to strike.

Penelope pulled her hand away from the crystal, her heart pounding. "I saw it. I saw the Lumen Blossom, but something else was there—a shadow. Something dangerous."

Jasper frowned. "A shadow? What kind of shadow?"

Penelope shook her head, her mind racing. "I don't know, but it's connected to the Lumen Blossom. Whatever it is, it's waiting for us."

The magic compass in Penelope's satchel began to glow softly, its needle pointing in the direction of the vision she had seen. It was as though the compass had sensed her discovery and was guiding her toward the next step of her journey.

"We need to leave," Penelope said, her voice firm. "We've seen what we needed to see. The Lumen Blossom is out there, and so is the danger. But now we know where to go."

Jasper nodded, his eyes wide with anticipation. "Then let's get moving. The sooner we find that blossom, the sooner we can figure out what this shadow is."

With the vision of the Lumen Blossom fresh in her mind, Penelope and Jasper made their way back through the Crystal Cavern, the glowing crystals around them pulsing softly as if bidding them farewell. The cavern had shown Penelope the many futures that lay before her, but now she was more determined than ever to create the one where she succeeded.

As they stepped out of the cavern and into the light of day, Penelope glanced down at the magic compass, which pointed steadily in the direction of their next adventure. The path ahead was still uncertain, and the dangers were growing, but Penelope knew that she had the strength to face whatever came next.

With renewed determination, Penelope and Jasper set off toward the final leg of their journey—the quest for the Lumen Blossom and the shadow that awaited them.

Chapter 22: The Portal of Wonder

The crisp mountain air swirled around Penelope as she and Jasper made their way down from the Crystal Cavern. The vision of the Lumen Blossom still lingered in her mind—the magical flower that held the key to saving the Butterfly Kingdom, and the ominous shadow that lurked nearby. As they journeyed deeper into the forest, following the steady guidance of the magic compass, Penelope felt a strange pull, as if something else was waiting for her, just out of sight.

The enchanted map had led her through many challenges, but now, it was the magic compass that guided her, its needle glowing softly and pointing toward an unknown destination. They walked for hours, the forest around them growing denser and quieter with each passing step. The compass led them toward a small clearing at the base of a hill, and there, shimmering faintly in the soft light, was something extraordinary.

It was a portal.

The portal stood tall, an oval of shimmering light that rippled like water. It was surrounded by twisting vines and ancient stones, and the air around it hummed with energy. The light from the portal shifted constantly, its colors blending and swirling in mesmerizing patterns of gold, blue, and violet.

Penelope's breath caught in her throat. "What is that?"

Jasper, who had been perched on her shoulder, leaped down to get a closer look. "It looks like some kind of... gateway. But where does it go?"

Penelope stepped forward cautiously, feeling the strange, magnetic pull of the portal's energy. The magic compass in her hand spun rapidly, its needle glowing brighter as if urging her forward. There was no doubt in her mind—this portal was important. But where it led, and what awaited on the other side, was a complete mystery.

"It's a portal to another dimension," Penelope whispered, her eyes wide with wonder. "A place where the rules of our world don't apply."

Jasper gave her a wary look. "I'm all for adventure, but are you sure about this? What if we step through and everything's upside down—or worse?"

Penelope hesitated, but the magic compass's steady glow reassured her. She had faced danger before, and every challenge had brought her closer to her goal. Whatever this portal led to, she knew it was part of her journey.

"I have to see what's on the other side," Penelope said, her voice resolute. "It's part of the path—maybe even part of finding the Lumen Blossom."

Jasper sighed, but nodded. "Alright, if you're going, I'm going with you. But let's be ready for anything."

Taking a deep breath, Penelope reached out and touched the surface of the portal. The shimmering light rippled beneath her fingers like liquid, warm and inviting. With a final glance at Jasper, she stepped through.

The moment Penelope passed through the portal, the world around her changed completely. The air felt lighter, almost weightless, and the colors of the landscape shifted in vibrant, impossible hues. She looked down and realized she was standing on a floating island—an island suspended in mid-air, with no ground below, only an endless sky filled with swirling clouds in shades of pink, orange, and violet.

Jasper appeared beside her, his eyes wide in disbelief. "What... where are we?"

Penelope looked around, her heart pounding with awe. The sky was unlike anything she had ever seen—alive with glowing trails of light that crisscrossed the sky like rivers of magic. The floating islands around them were covered in strange, glowing plants and trees that shimmered like stars, their leaves sparkling in every color of the rainbow.

"It's like we've stepped into a dream," Penelope whispered, her voice filled with wonder. "This place doesn't follow the rules of nature. Everything here is different—almost... magical."

As they walked across the floating island, Penelope noticed that the ground beneath their feet felt soft, like walking on air. In the distance, she could see other floating islands drifting lazily through the sky, connected by delicate bridges made of light. The air was filled with the sound of distant, melodic music, as though the dimension itself was singing.

"I've never seen anything like this," Jasper said, his voice filled with awe. "It's like the whole world is alive with magic."

Penelope nodded, her eyes scanning the horizon. "But why are we here? What is this place trying to show us?"

As they continued to explore, Penelope's eyes were drawn to a structure on one of the nearby islands—a tall, shimmering tower made entirely of crystal. It glowed with a soft, golden light, and Penelope felt an irresistible pull toward it.

"The compass is pointing toward that tower," Penelope said, holding up the glowing compass. "I think that's where we need to go."

Jasper nodded, his eyes wide with excitement. "Then let's find a way to get there."

They made their way across the floating islands, hopping over glowing bridges of light and navigating pathways that twisted and spiralled through the sky. The more they explored, the more Penelope realized that this dimension was alive with its own unique magic—a magic that defied the laws of nature she had always known.

At one point, Penelope stepped onto a patch of glowing flowers, and to her amazement, they lifted her into the air, carrying her gently across a gap between the islands. Jasper followed, clinging tightly to her shoulder as they floated across the sky, the flowers moving gracefully beneath them.

"This place just keeps getting stranger," Jasper muttered, his tail flicking nervously. "But I'll admit, it's pretty amazing."

When they finally reached the island with the crystal tower, Penelope felt a surge of anticipation. The tower glowed with a brilliant golden light, its walls reflecting the swirling colors of the sky. As they approached the entrance, Penelope noticed that the door was made of the same shimmering material as the portal they had passed through.

"This must be where the answers are," Penelope said, her heart racing. "There's something inside the tower that we're meant to find."

With a deep breath, Penelope pushed open the door and stepped inside.

The interior of the tower was breathtaking. The walls were lined with thousands of glowing crystals, each one pulsing with light. At the center of the room was a large, circular pool of water, its surface shimmering like liquid gold. The pool seemed to ripple with energy, and as Penelope approached, she saw something extraordinary.

Reflected in the water were not just her own face and Jasper's, but countless versions of herself—each one slightly different. Some showed her standing in a vast forest, holding the Lumen Blossom. Others showed her sailing the skies aboard the Stormrider, or facing down unknown dangers with bravery and resolve. There were also darker reflections—futures where she stood alone, lost or afraid, with shadows creeping at the edges of the visions.

Penelope's breath caught in her throat. "It's like the crystals in the cavern... they're showing me possible futures."

Jasper leaned closer to the pool, his eyes wide. "But this time, they're more... real. It's like you're seeing all the paths you could take."

Penelope stared at the reflections, her mind racing. Every choice she had made, every decision she had yet to make, was reflected in the pool. The futures were infinite, and each one depended on the path she chose moving forward. But as she studied the reflections, her eyes were drawn to one in particular—a version of herself standing at the base of a large, glowing tree, its branches covered in delicate, radiant flowers.

"The Lumen Blossom," Penelope whispered. "It's part of my future, but I have to choose the right path."

The reflection shifted, and Penelope saw herself facing the shadow she had seen in the crystal cavern—a tall, ominous figure with glowing eyes, shrouded in darkness. The shadow was connected to the Lumen Blossom, and she knew that to find the flower, she would also have to confront this lurking danger.

Jasper, sensing her unease, placed a paw on her arm. "Whatever path you choose, we'll face it together."

Penelope smiled, feeling a wave of determination wash over her. "Thank you, Jasper. I know we can do this."

As she stepped away from the pool, the magic compass in her satchel pulsed, its needle glowing brighter than ever. It was pointing directly toward the vision of the glowing tree—the path that led to the Lumen Blossom. With renewed purpose, Penelope knew that the portal had shown her what she needed to see. The laws of nature were different here, but the choices she made, and the path she chose, remained hers to control.

"We've seen what we needed to see," Penelope said, turning to Jasper. "Let's head back. We have a Lumen Blossom to find."

Jasper grinned, and together, they made their way back through the portal. The world of floating islands and glowing lights faded behind them as they returned to the familiar forest, the magic compass now guiding them forward with a clear purpose.

As they stepped back into their own world, Penelope felt a sense of clarity. The portal had revealed a glimpse of what lay ahead, and now, armed with that knowledge, she was ready to face whatever challenges awaited.

The journey wasn't over, but with the compass and her own determination, Penelope knew that the path to the Lumen Blossom—and the truth behind the shadow—was within reach.

Chapter 23: The Lost Library

After their journey through the Portal of Wonder, Penelope and Jasper returned to the familiar embrace of the forest. The magic compass still guided them, its steady glow leading them toward the final steps of their quest—the search for the Lumen Blossom and the truth behind the ominous shadow. But as they ventured deeper into the woods, something unexpected caught Penelope's eye.

They had wandered into an ancient part of the forest, where the trees were taller, their bark gnarled and twisted with age. The leaves above created a canopy so thick that only faint beams of light filtered through. There was a stillness in the air, as though time itself had forgotten this place. And then, through the mist, Penelope saw it: a grand, crumbling building hidden among the trees.

The structure was unlike anything Penelope had seen before. It was made of dark, weathered stone, with tall arched windows that had long since been overtaken by vines and moss. The building looked as though it had been abandoned for centuries, yet there was something magical about it, something that whispered to her, urging her to come closer.

Jasper, perched on Penelope's shoulder, squinted at the building. "Is that... a library?"

Penelope nodded slowly. "It looks like one. But what's a library doing in the middle of the forest?"

They approached cautiously, their footsteps soft on the moss-covered ground. As they neared the entrance, Penelope saw an inscription carved into the stone above the doorway. The letters were old and worn, but she could still make out the words:

"The Lost Library of Eldergreen."

Penelope's heart skipped a beat. The name sounded familiar, though she couldn't recall where she had heard it. She pushed open the heavy wooden doors, which creaked loudly, and stepped inside. The moment they crossed the threshold, the air changed. It was warmer here, almost inviting, and the smell of ancient books and dust filled Penelope's senses.

Inside, the library was enormous. Shelves upon shelves of books stretched up toward the ceiling, which was so high it disappeared into shadows. The walls were lined with books of every size and color, and ladders stood in each corner, reaching toward the highest shelves. But there was something different about this library—something Penelope couldn't quite put into words.

"Wow..." Jasper muttered, his eyes wide as he took in the scene. "This place is huge. How long do you think it's been here?"

Penelope shook her head. "I don't know. But I think we're about to find out."

As they wandered deeper into the library, Penelope noticed something strange. The books weren't still. They moved, their pages fluttering as though they were breathing, and some of them glowed faintly with magic. The shelves hummed with energy, and Penelope could feel the weight of the forest's history pressing down on her. These weren't just ordinary books—these books were alive.

Jasper, noticing the movement, gave a nervous laugh. "Is it just me, or are the books... watching us?"

Penelope smiled, but there was a hint of nervousness in her voice. "I think they are."

She reached out cautiously to one of the books on a nearby shelf. The cover was made of soft, worn leather, and the title, written in gold script, read: "The Story of the Whispering Tree."

The moment Penelope touched the book, it sprang to life. The pages flipped open of their own accord, and the book hovered in the air before her, glowing softly. The words on the pages began to change, shifting and rearranging themselves until they formed a coherent story. But this wasn't just any story—it was a story Penelope recognized.

The book began to speak, its voice soft and melodic, as if the forest itself were telling the tale. "Long ago, in the heart of the Eldergreen

Forest, there stood a tree unlike any other. Its roots ran deep into the earth, and its branches reached for the stars. This was the Whispering Tree, a keeper of secrets, whose leaves whispered the truths of the land to those who would listen..."

Penelope's eyes widened. "That's the tree I found! The one that gave me the enchanted map."

The book continued, its voice growing softer, more personal. "The tree sensed the presence of a seeker—one who was curious and kind, with a heart full of wonder. To this seeker, the tree gifted a map, one that would guide her through the forest and beyond, toward the greatest adventure of all."

Penelope felt a shiver run down her spine. The book wasn't just telling her the history of the forest—it was telling her story. The book knew who she was.

Jasper blinked in astonishment. "It's like the forest remembers everything you've done."

Penelope nodded, still in awe. "These books... they're alive with the stories of the forest. They hold its history, and now they're telling us the parts that matter."

Curiosity overtook her, and Penelope moved to another shelf, where another book caught her eye. This one was larger, bound in deep green leather, with the title: "The Tale of the Butterfly Kingdom."

When she touched it, the book floated into the air, and its pages flipped open, revealing the story of the kingdom she had been fighting to save. The voice that spoke was different this time—softer, more delicate, like the fluttering of butterfly wings.

"Once, in the heart of the Eldergreen Forest, there was a kingdom of light and beauty. The butterflies that lived there were sentient, their wings sparkling like jewels in the sun. They ruled their land with grace, sharing their magic with the forest and its creatures. But a darkness began to spread, a shadow that threatened to extinguish their light. The kingdom's queen, wise and kind, sought a way to protect her people..."

Penelope's heart raced as she listened to the story. The book continued, describing the queen's search for the Lumen Blossom, a flower with the power to restore life and light to the kingdom. But before the queen could find it, the darkness overtook her, freezing the kingdom in time.

"That's the curse," Penelope whispered. "The Lumen Blossom is the only thing that can save them."

Jasper nodded solemnly. "But it sounds like the queen didn't get to it in time. We have to make sure we do."

As they moved from shelf to shelf, Penelope realized that each book held a personal story, not just about the forest, but about her own journey through it. Some books told of places she had yet to visit, of dangers and wonders still ahead. Others told of allies she had met, like Jasper, Captain Marlowe, and the sky pirates. Each story was a piece of the puzzle, a fragment of the forest's living history.

But then, Penelope spotted a book unlike the others. It was small and unassuming, its cover plain and worn, with no title. Something about it drew her in, and when she touched it, the book didn't float like the others. Instead, it remained in her hands, the pages heavy with untold secrets.

Penelope opened the book, and her breath caught in her throat. Inside were no words—only images. Drawn in delicate ink, the pages showed scenes of her journey, but there were also strange, shadowy figures lurking at the edges of each picture. And in the final image, there was a dark figure standing beside the Lumen Blossom, its hand reaching out toward the flower.

Penelope's heart raced. "This is the shadow... the one from my vision."

Jasper peered over her shoulder. "That's it! That's the thing we saw in the Crystal Cavern."

Penelope felt a chill run down her spine. The shadow had been following her, lingering at the edges of her journey, waiting for her to find the Lumen Blossom. But what did it want? Why was it connected to the flower?

"We need to be ready," Penelope said quietly, closing the book. "Whatever this shadow is, it's going to be there when we find the Lumen Blossom."

Jasper nodded, his eyes wide with concern. "And we'll face it together."

Penelope placed the book back on the shelf, her mind swirling with thoughts. The Lost Library had shown her the history of the forest, but it had also revealed the truth about her own journey. The Lumen Blossom was close, but so was the danger that accompanied it.

As they made their way back to the entrance of the library, Penelope felt a renewed sense of purpose. The forest's stories were alive, and now she was part of that history. The magic compass pulsed softly in her satchel, its needle pointing steadily toward the next adventure.

With the knowledge from the Lost Library fresh in her mind, Penelope and Jasper stepped out into the forest once more, ready to face whatever came next. The journey to the Lumen Blossom was nearly at an end—but the most difficult challenge was still to come.

Chapter 24: The Mirror of Illusions

Penelope and Jasper had left the Lost Library of Eldergreen with a new sense of urgency. The stories they had uncovered—the whispered histories of the forest and the personal tales of her journey—had shown her how close she was to finding the Lumen Blossom. But they had also revealed the looming presence of the shadow, a threat she couldn't ignore. As they followed the magic compass deeper into the heart of the forest, Penelope felt the weight of her choices bearing down on her.

The trees around them grew taller and denser, their branches twisting overhead like a living canopy. The forest floor was soft underfoot, the air cool and tinged with the scent of moss and pine. The magic compass pulsed in Penelope's hand, its needle pointing steadily forward, but something else was drawing her attention—a faint glimmer of light shining through the trees.

"What's that?" Jasper asked, hopping down from her shoulder to get a better look.

Penelope frowned, following the strange light. "I don't know, but it feels... familiar."

They pushed through the underbrush, and soon, they found themselves standing before something unexpected: a tall, ornate mirror. It was framed in silver, its surface smooth and polished, glowing faintly in the soft light of the forest. The mirror was out of place among the trees, like a relic of another world.

Penelope approached cautiously, her eyes wide with curiosity. "A mirror? Out here?"

Jasper tilted his head. "This forest is full of surprises, but I've never seen anything like this."

The mirror stood still, almost inviting, and Penelope couldn't resist the urge to step closer. As she did, her reflection appeared clearly in the glass. But something was different—this wasn't just an ordinary mirror.

The reflection didn't just show her as she was—it showed her as she could be.

Penelope stared into the mirror, and her breath caught in her throat. Her reflection shifted and changed, showing alternate versions of herself. In one image, she stood tall and confident, holding the Lumen Blossom high above her head, her face filled with triumph. In another, she was dressed in the garb of a sky pirate, sailing through the clouds with Captain Marlowe and his crew, her eyes gleaming with adventure. Yet another reflection showed her standing before a shadowy figure, her expression serious and determined, as though preparing for a final battle.

"These are... different versions of me," Penelope whispered, her heart racing. "They're showing what I could become."

Jasper blinked, his tiny paws twitching nervously. "Are these your future selves?"

Penelope studied the reflections closely. Each version of herself seemed to embody a different aspect of her potential—a brave adventurer, a wise leader, a fierce protector. But there were also darker versions—reflections that showed her lost, unsure, or afraid. In one reflection, she stood alone in the middle of a dark, twisting forest, her face shadowed with uncertainty. In another, she was surrounded by swirling mist, the shadowy figure looming over her as if to claim victory.

Penelope's heart pounded as she tried to make sense of it all. "It's like the mirror is showing me who I could be... depending on the choices I make."

Jasper hopped closer, his eyes wide with wonder. "But why? Why would the forest want you to see this?"

Penelope didn't know, but she felt a deep connection to the mirror's magic. It wasn't trying to scare her—it was trying to help her understand something important about herself. Every reflection she saw was a possibility, a path she could take. The forest had given her this mirror not to show her what would happen, but to show her what could happen, depending on her choices.

She placed her hand on the cool surface of the mirror, and in that instant, a new reflection appeared. This time, it showed Penelope standing at the edge of a cliff, holding the Lumen Blossom in her hands. But she wasn't alone. The shadowy figure from her visions was there, too, watching her from the darkness. It didn't move, but its presence was overwhelming, as if waiting for the moment to strike.

Penelope pulled her hand back, her heart racing. "The shadow... it's tied to the Lumen Blossom somehow. I have to face it when I find the flower."

Jasper nodded solemnly. "But you're strong, Penelope. You've made it this far. You'll figure out how to beat it."

Penelope smiled at Jasper's encouragement, but the weight of the reflections lingered in her mind. The mirror had shown her the many paths her future could take, and now it was up to her to choose the one that would lead to success. She understood now that every step she took mattered—every decision shaped the person she was becoming.

As she turned away from the mirror, she felt a strange sense of clarity. The mirror hadn't just shown her possible futures—it had shown her who she already was. A girl filled with curiosity, courage, and determination. Someone who had faced incredible challenges and grown stronger with each one. And someone who would have to trust in herself to face the final test ahead.

"This mirror... it's not just about showing me the future," Penelope said quietly. "It's showing me that I have the power to shape my own story."

Jasper grinned. "You always have, Penelope. You've been writing this adventure all along."

With a renewed sense of purpose, Penelope glanced back at the magic compass. Its needle glowed brightly, pointing toward the next destination with unwavering certainty. The Mirror of Illusions had revealed her true potential, and now, she knew that no matter what the future held, she had the strength to face it.

"We need to keep going," Penelope said, her voice filled with resolve. "The Lumen Blossom is waiting, and so is the shadow. But whatever happens, I'm ready."

Jasper nodded enthusiastically. "And I'll be with you every step of the way."

As they left the clearing, the mirror remained behind, glowing softly in the forest's shadows. It had served its purpose, showing Penelope the infinite possibilities ahead of her. Now, she had to take the knowledge it had given her and move forward—toward the Lumen Blossom, the shadow, and the final challenge that awaited.

With the compass guiding their way and the reflection of her true potential fresh in her mind, Penelope felt more determined than ever. The adventure was nearing its end, but the most important part was still ahead. And whatever the outcome, she knew that she had the strength to write her own story—one filled with courage, kindness, and hope.

Chapter 25: The Beast of the Mountains

The air had grown colder as Penelope and Jasper ventured further into the forest, the magic compass still guiding them. The mirror's revelations were fresh in Penelope's mind, and though the path ahead was uncertain, she felt a deep sense of resolve. She was closer to finding the Lumen Blossom, but the journey had taken them near the foot of a towering mountain range, where a new mystery awaited.

As they walked, Penelope noticed a faint trail of smoke rising in the distance. It came from a small village nestled in the shadow of the mountains, its thatched roofs and stone cottages standing stark against the jagged peaks. But something about the village seemed off—the air was tense, and there was no sound of activity or movement.

"Something's wrong," Penelope said, her brow furrowed. "Let's go check it out."

Jasper nodded, his small face serious. "Maybe they've seen the shadow, or worse—something's happened to the people here."

As they approached the village, Penelope saw that the homes were intact, but the streets were empty, as if everyone had retreated indoors. She knocked on the door of the nearest cottage, but no one answered. Instead, a small, frightened face appeared in a nearby window—a young boy peering out nervously.

Penelope smiled reassuringly and waved for him to come outside. After a moment's hesitation, the boy opened the door just enough to poke his head through.

"Who are you?" he asked in a trembling voice. "You shouldn't be here. The beast might come back."

Penelope's heart skipped a beat. "The beast?"

The boy nodded quickly. "It lives in the mountains. It's been terrorizing our village for weeks—stealing food, scaring people away. No one knows what to do."

Jasper frowned, his ears twitching. "A beast in the mountains? That sounds serious. Have you seen it?"

The boy shook his head. "Not up close. People say it's huge, with sharp claws and glowing eyes. But no one's gotten close enough to see for sure. My father says it'll destroy the whole village if we don't stop it soon."

Penelope exchanged a glance with Jasper. Something about this didn't sit right. A creature that had been terrorizing the village, but no one had seen it clearly? It reminded her of the stories she'd heard before—of misunderstood creatures labelled as monsters because people were too afraid to understand them.

"Do you know where the beast lives?" Penelope asked gently.

The boy hesitated, then pointed toward the mountain range. "There's a cave, up high on the ridge. That's where people say it comes from. But it's dangerous to go up there. My father says it's a place of bad magic."

Penelope knelt down so she was at eye level with the boy. "Don't worry. We'll check it out, and we'll make sure no one else gets hurt. You're very brave for telling us."

The boy's eyes widened in surprise. "You're really going up there? But the beast—"

Penelope smiled warmly. "We'll be careful. And we'll figure out what's going on."

With the boy's directions in mind, Penelope and Jasper set off toward the mountains. The rocky path was steep and treacherous, but Penelope's determination pushed her forward. As they climbed higher, the wind grew colder, and the landscape became more barren, the trees thinning out until only jagged rocks remained.

"I don't like this," Jasper muttered, his eyes scanning the ridge ahead. "If the stories are true, we're walking right into the beast's lair."

Penelope nodded, but there was something tugging at her instincts. The stories didn't add up. If the creature had been attacking the village, why hadn't anyone seen it clearly? And why hadn't it done more damage?

As they neared the top of the ridge, a large cave came into view, its entrance dark and foreboding. Penelope took a deep breath, steeling herself for what might come next.

"This is it," she said softly. "Stay close."

Jasper hopped onto her shoulder, his small paws gripping her cloak tightly. "Let's hope this beast isn't as scary as everyone says."

They stepped cautiously into the cave, the air inside cool and damp. The light from the entrance faded quickly, leaving only the faint glow of the enchanted map to guide them. As they ventured deeper into the cave, Penelope heard a soft sound—like breathing, slow and rhythmic, coming from further ahead.

Her heart pounded in her chest as she rounded a corner and found herself in a large, open chamber. There, at the center of the cave, was the beast.

It was large, no doubt about that—its massive form curled up on the floor of the cave, its head resting on its paws. Its fur was thick and shaggy, dark as the shadows around it, and its eyes glowed faintly in the dim light. But what surprised Penelope most was that the creature didn't look fearsome at all. In fact, it looked... sad.

The beast stirred slightly, lifting its head to look at them. Penelope held her breath, expecting it to growl or attack, but instead, it just stared at them with tired, golden eyes.

"It's... not attacking," Jasper whispered, his voice filled with disbelief.

Penelope took a cautious step forward. "Hello?" she called softly. "We don't want to hurt you. We just want to understand why you've been scaring the village."

The beast blinked slowly, then let out a low, rumbling sigh. Its eyes, though fierce-looking, held no malice—only sorrow.

Penelope's heart ached as she realized what was happening. "You're not a monster, are you? You're just... misunderstood."

The beast let out a soft growl, almost as if it were agreeing with her. It shifted slightly, and Penelope noticed that one of its back legs was injured—a deep gash running along its side, hidden beneath its thick fur.

"You're hurt," Penelope said, her voice filled with sympathy. "That's why you've been going to the village. You needed help."

Jasper frowned, his earlier fear giving way to concern. "The poor thing's probably been stealing food because it's too weak to hunt."

Penelope stepped closer, kneeling down beside the beast. "It's okay," she said softly. "We can help you."

To her surprise, the beast didn't shy away. Instead, it lowered its head, as if trusting her. Penelope gently examined the wound, and though it looked painful, it wasn't beyond healing. With some herbs and bandages, she could help it recover.

"We need to go back to the village and get supplies," Penelope said, turning to Jasper. "But we can't let them think the beast is dangerous."

Jasper nodded. "We'll explain everything. Once they know the truth, they'll understand."

They left the cave and hurried back down the mountain. When they returned to the village, Penelope went straight to the boy who had spoken to them earlier. His father, a tall, serious-looking man, stood nearby, his face filled with concern.

"You went up there?" the father asked, his brow furrowed. "Did you see the beast?"

Penelope nodded. "Yes, but it's not what you think. The beast isn't dangerous—it's hurt. That's why it's been coming down to the village. It's looking for food because it's too injured to hunt."

The father's eyes widened in surprise. "Hurt? But we thought—"

Penelope smiled gently. "I know it's scary, but the beast isn't a threat. It just needs help. If we can treat its injury, it won't bother the village anymore."

The boy stepped forward, his eyes shining with curiosity. "So it's not a monster?"

Penelope shook her head. "No, it's not. And with your help, we can make sure it gets better."

Moved by Penelope's compassion, the villagers gathered supplies—herbs, bandages, and food—and followed her back to the cave. When they arrived, the beast didn't react with fear or aggression. Instead, it lay still, allowing Penelope and the others to tend to its wound.

As they worked, the villagers' fear melted away, replaced by understanding. The beast, once thought to be a monster, was simply an injured creature in need of kindness.

Over the next few days, the beast grew stronger, and soon it was able to return to the mountains, where it could live peacefully, no longer needing to raid the village for food.

As Penelope and Jasper prepared to leave the village, the boy and his father came to say goodbye.

"Thank you for helping us," the father said, his voice filled with gratitude. "We were so afraid, but you showed us the truth. We'll never forget it."

Penelope smiled. "Sometimes, things aren't as scary as they seem. You just have to look a little closer."

With the beast safely healed and the village no longer in danger, Penelope and Jasper set off once again, the magic compass pointing them toward their next destination. The journey ahead was still full of unknowns, but Penelope knew one thing for sure—kindness and understanding could change everything, even in the face of fear.

Chapter 26: The Secret Underground

After helping the villagers and healing the misunderstood Beast of the Mountains, Penelope and Jasper continued their journey, the magic compass guiding them once again. The air felt lighter after the events in the village, but there was still a quiet sense of anticipation—Penelope knew that the Lumen Blossom and the shadow were drawing closer.

The magic compass glowed faintly in her hand, its needle pointing toward a dense part of the forest where the trees grew thick and the underbrush tangled together like a maze. As they moved through the towering trees, Penelope noticed something strange—a narrow path that seemed almost hidden beneath layers of leaves and moss, as though no one had walked it for centuries.

"I think the compass is leading us down there," Penelope said, glancing at Jasper, who had been sniffing around curiously.

Jasper flicked his tail, his eyes sharp. "Looks like no one's been here in a long time. Maybe it's hiding something important."

They carefully followed the hidden path, pushing aside branches and stepping over roots that had grown wild. The deeper they went, the more the forest seemed to change. The trees became darker, their branches twisting in strange patterns, and the air was cooler, almost damp. Then, as they rounded a bend, Penelope spotted something unusual—a large stone door, half-hidden beneath a mound of earth and overgrown vines.

The door was carved with intricate symbols, swirling designs that seemed to glow faintly in the dim light. Penelope's heart raced as she reached out and brushed the vines aside, revealing an ancient inscription carved into the stone:

"The Guardians of Eldergreen Protect the Secret of the Forest."

Penelope's eyes widened. "The Guardians of Eldergreen... I've heard that name before. The Lost Library mentioned them."

Jasper hopped closer, peering at the door. "Guardians? Do you think they're still here?"

Penelope studied the inscription, her mind racing. The Guardians must have been some kind of ancient protectors, keeping the secrets of the forest hidden from those who weren't meant to find them. But what secret were they guarding? And why had this place been forgotten for so long?

There was only one way to find out.

Penelope pressed her hand against the stone door. At first, nothing happened, but then, slowly, the door began to rumble and shift, sliding open to reveal a dark passageway leading underground. A cool draft of air flowed out, carrying with it the faint scent of earth and stone.

Penelope glanced at Jasper, her heart pounding. "This is it. We're going underground."

Jasper twitched his nose, his eyes wide with excitement. "Let's see what these Guardians are hiding."

Together, they stepped through the doorway and descended into the hidden passage. The stone walls were rough, carved with more of the swirling symbols that glowed faintly as they walked deeper into the underground. The air was cool and damp, and Penelope could hear the faint sound of water dripping somewhere in the distance.

The passage wound downward, spiralling deeper into the earth, until finally, they emerged into a vast underground chamber. Penelope gasped. Before her was an entire underground city, hidden beneath the forest. Towering stone buildings lined the walls, their surfaces covered in glowing moss and shimmering crystals that illuminated the space. Bridges of stone and wood crisscrossed overhead, connecting the buildings, and the sound of flowing water echoed through the chamber.

But what caught Penelope's attention most were the creatures.

They were unlike any she had ever seen before. Some were small and delicate, with wings made of gossamer and eyes that shimmered like jewels. Others were larger, with fur or scales, their bodies blending seamlessly into the shadows. All of them moved quietly, going about their lives in the underground city, but when they saw Penelope and Jasper, they paused, watching curiously.

"These... these must be the forgotten creatures," Penelope whispered, her eyes wide with wonder. "The Guardians of Eldergreen."

Jasper's eyes darted around. "I've never seen creatures like these. What are they doing down here?"

Penelope felt a sense of awe wash over her as she realized the truth. These creatures had been hidden from the world for centuries, living in secret beneath the forest, guarding something important—something vital to the forest's survival. The inscription on the door had said they were protecting the secret of the forest. But what was it?

As Penelope and Jasper stepped further into the city, one of the creatures approached them. It was tall and graceful, with silvery skin and glowing eyes that reflected the light of the crystals. It bowed slightly, its voice soft and melodic as it spoke.

"Welcome, traveller," the creature said. "You have found the city of the Guardians. Few have ventured this far, and fewer still are worthy to know the secret we protect."

Penelope's heart raced. "What is this place? What secret are you guarding?"

The creature tilted its head, studying her carefully. "We are the last of the ancient creatures, bound to this place by the magic of the forest. For centuries, we have protected the life force of Eldergreen, the magic that sustains the forest and all who live within it."

"The life force?" Penelope asked, her voice filled with wonder.

The creature nodded. "Yes. The magic that flows through the trees, the rivers, and the creatures of the forest. Without it, the forest would wither and die. It is a magic as old as the earth itself, and it is our duty to guard it."

Penelope felt a shiver run down her spine. This was the secret that had been hidden for so long—the life force that sustained the forest. It wasn't just a magical place; it was alive, its magic connected to everything within it.

"But why has it been hidden for so long?" Penelope asked. "Why haven't the people of the forest been told about this?"

The creature's expression grew sombre. "Long ago, there were those who sought to use the life force for their own gain. They believed they could control it, harness its power to bend the forest to their will. But such attempts only brought destruction and imbalance. And so, we hid the life force away, deep beneath the earth, where only the worthy could find it."

Penelope nodded, understanding now. The Guardians had been protecting the forest from those who would exploit its magic. But something else still nagged at her—the shadow she had seen in her visions, the one tied to the Lumen Blossom.

"There's something else," Penelope said, her voice hesitant. "I've been searching for the Lumen Blossom—a flower with the power to restore life. But I've seen visions of a shadow, something dark that's connected to it. Do you know what it is?"

The creature's glowing eyes flickered, and it stepped closer, its voice lowering. "The Lumen Blossom is indeed connected to the life force of the forest. It is the physical manifestation of the forest's power to heal and renew. But the shadow you speak of... that is the darkness that seeks to consume the life force. It is an ancient curse, born from the greed of those who once tried to control the magic. The shadow has lingered for centuries, waiting for someone to disturb the balance."

Penelope's heart sank. The shadow was a threat not just to the Lumen Blossom, but to the entire forest. If it succeeded in consuming the life force, the forest would die, and everything within it would be lost.

"I have to stop it," Penelope said, her voice filled with determination. "The shadow can't be allowed to destroy the forest."

The creature nodded solemnly. "You are brave, young traveller, and you may be the one to restore balance to the forest. The Lumen Blossom is the key. But beware—the shadow will not give up easily. It will try to twist your path, to make you doubt yourself. You must remain strong."

Penelope took a deep breath, the weight of her task settling on her shoulders. The journey had led her to this moment, and now she knew what she had to do. The Lumen Blossom held the power to save the forest, but the shadow would be waiting for her, ready to claim the life force for itself.

"We'll stop it," Penelope said firmly. "No matter what."

The creature smiled softly, its eyes glowing with hope. "Then go, and may the magic of Eldergreen guide you. The Lumen Blossom awaits, and so does your destiny."

With renewed purpose, Penelope and Jasper left the underground city, the weight of the forest's secret now resting on their shoulders. The magic compass pointed steadily ahead, leading them toward the final leg of their journey.

As they emerged back into the light of the forest, Penelope felt a sense of clarity. The Guardians had entrusted her with the most important task of all—to protect the life force of the forest. And she would do whatever it took to ensure the balance was restored.

The Lumen Blossom was within reach, but so was the shadow. And Penelope knew that the greatest challenge of her adventure was still ahead.

Chapter 27: The Whisper of the Wind

The forest stretched out before Penelope and Jasper as they left the underground city behind. The revelations from the Guardians of Eldergreen weighed heavily on her mind. The Lumen Blossom and the shadow were part of something much bigger—the life force of the forest itself. And now, Penelope knew the stakes were higher than ever. But even as she felt the weight of her task, something in the forest air was shifting, as if the very wind had a message for her.

The magic compass pulsed faintly in her hand, its needle pointing forward as always, but now there was something different. The wind itself seemed to swirl around Penelope, tugging at her cloak and whispering in her ears. It wasn't just a normal breeze—this wind had a voice, though faint, and it seemed to be calling her.

"Do you feel that?" Penelope asked Jasper, her voice barely above a whisper.

Jasper flicked his ears, his nose twitching in the breeze. "Yeah... it's like the wind is trying to tell us something. But I can't understand it."

Penelope closed her eyes for a moment, letting the wind swirl around her. The breeze seemed to dance between the trees, rushing through the leaves and rustling the grass. It carried with it a soft, melodic whisper—words that Penelope couldn't quite make out, but she knew they were there.

She opened her eyes, her heart racing. "I think the wind is speaking to me."

Jasper blinked. "The wind? Can you understand it?"

Penelope shook her head. "Not fully, but I think it's trying to guide us. Maybe... maybe it knows where we need to go next."

The thought seemed strange at first, but the more Penelope thought about it, the more sense it made. The forest was alive, and the wind was part of that life. It moved through the trees, carrying whispers of ancient magic, and perhaps it could guide her to places that even the enchanted map and the magic compass couldn't reach.

Penelope took a deep breath and decided to trust the wind. "Let's follow it," she said, her voice filled with quiet determination. "The wind knows something we don't."

Jasper gave a cautious nod. "If you say so. I just hope we're not walking into a trap."

The wind swirled around them again, this time tugging gently at Penelope's cloak, as if urging her forward. She followed its lead, stepping off the path and into a part of the forest she hadn't explored before. The trees here were tall and twisted, their branches reaching high into the sky, and the ground was uneven, covered in moss and thick roots. But the wind never wavered, its whisper guiding Penelope deeper into the heart of the forest.

As they walked, Penelope listened carefully, trying to make sense of the wind's voice. At first, it was nothing more than a faint murmur, like the rustling of leaves in a soft breeze. But slowly, the words became clearer, forming a gentle melody that danced on the air.

"Follow… the wind… to where only the sky can see," the whisper said, the voice as soft as the wind itself.

Penelope's eyes widened. "I think… I think it's telling us to go higher. Somewhere only the sky can see."

Jasper glanced up at the towering trees around them. "Higher? Like, up the mountain again?"

Penelope nodded, her heart pounding with anticipation. "I think so. There's something waiting for us at the top. Something we can only find if we let the wind guide us."

They continued their journey, the wind's voice growing stronger as they climbed higher into the hills. The path became steeper, and the trees thinned out, giving way to rocky cliffs and open skies. The wind whipped around them, carrying with it the scent of pine and earth, and Penelope felt a strange sense of exhilaration. She was walking a path that only the wind knew, and each step brought her closer to something magical.

As they reached a ridge that overlooked the forest below, the wind's whisper grew louder, more urgent. Penelope stopped, her breath catching in her throat as she looked out over the vast expanse of trees and valleys. The view was breathtaking, but what caught her attention most was a narrow ledge that jutted out from the cliffside—a place where only the wind could reach.

"That's it," Penelope said softly, pointing to the ledge. "The wind wants us to go there."

Jasper's eyes widened. "There? But it's so narrow. How are we supposed to get across?"

Penelope studied the ledge carefully. It was precarious, but there was a way across if they were careful. The wind seemed to be guiding them, whispering softly in her ears, encouraging her to take the leap.

"I think we can do it," Penelope said, her voice steady. "The wind is showing us the way. We just have to trust it."

With a deep breath, Penelope stepped onto the narrow ledge, her heart pounding in her chest. The wind swirled around her, gentle yet insistent, as if it were guiding her feet along the path. Jasper followed closely behind, his small paws moving cautiously along the rocky surface.

As they reached the center of the ledge, Penelope felt a strange sensation, as though the wind itself was lifting her, carrying her forward. She glanced down, and to her amazement, the ground seemed to shimmer beneath her feet, the rocks glowing faintly with a soft blue light. It was as if the wind had unlocked a hidden magic in the earth, revealing a path that only those who could hear its voice could walk.

"Look at that," Jasper whispered, his eyes wide with wonder. "The wind is... helping us."

Penelope smiled, her heart filled with awe. "It's part of the magic of the forest. The wind is alive, just like everything else here."

They continued along the ledge, the wind's voice growing softer but more reassuring with each step. When they reached the end of the ledge, they found themselves standing before a small, hidden grove nestled against the cliffside. The grove was filled with tall, graceful trees whose leaves shimmered in the sunlight, and in the center of the grove stood a stone altar.

On the altar was a small, glowing object—another piece of the puzzle that Penelope had been searching for.

"It's a wind crystal," Penelope whispered, stepping closer to the altar. The crystal pulsed softly with the same energy she had felt in the wind, its light glowing with a pale blue hue. "This must be what the wind was leading us to."

Jasper hopped closer, his eyes gleaming with excitement. "Do you think it's connected to the Lumen Blossom? Or maybe it'll help us understand more about the forest's magic?"

Penelope picked up the wind crystal, feeling its cool energy pulse through her fingers. The moment she touched it, the wind around them stilled, as if it had fulfilled its purpose. The magic compass in her hand glowed softly, its needle pointing forward once more, but now it seemed clearer than ever—the wind had guided them to this place for a reason.

"The wind led us here because we needed this crystal," Penelope said, her voice filled with understanding. "It's part of the forest's magic, just like the life force we learned about from the Guardians. This crystal holds the power of the wind—the power to guide, to protect, and to reach places no one else can."

Jasper grinned. "And now it's ours. Looks like we're one step closer to finding the Lumen Blossom."

Penelope smiled, tucking the wind crystal safely into her satchel. The wind had whispered its secrets to her, and now she knew that its power would be with her for the rest of her journey.

As they made their way back down the mountain, Penelope felt a sense of peace. The wind had shown her a new part of the forest's magic, and she had learned to listen to its voice. With the wind crystal in her possession, she knew she was closer than ever to finding the Lumen Blossom—and stopping the shadow that threatened to consume the forest.

But for now, Penelope was content to let the wind carry her forward, knowing that wherever it led, she was ready to follow.

Chapter 28: The Guardians of the Forest

The sun was beginning to set, casting long shadows across the forest floor as Penelope and Jasper made their way through the trees. The wind crystal, now safely tucked into Penelope's satchel, pulsed softly with energy, its magic blending with the forest around them. After learning to understand the whisper of the wind, Penelope felt more attuned to the forest than ever before. But even as the wind guided her, she knew the journey wasn't over—there was something else waiting for her deeper in the woods.

As the magic compass glowed steadily in her hand, pointing them forward, the air around them seemed to change. The trees grew taller and more ancient, their bark twisted and covered in thick moss. The canopy above was dense, allowing only slivers of light to filter through, casting the forest in a twilight glow. There was a sense of power here, as though the forest itself was watching, waiting.

"We're getting close to something," Penelope said softly, glancing at Jasper, who had been unusually quiet.

Jasper nodded, his eyes scanning the trees. "I feel it too. The air's different here, like the forest is alive in a way it hasn't been before."

They continued walking, the path narrowing as they ventured deeper into the heart of the forest. Soon, they came to a small clearing, and at the center of the clearing stood a circle of towering, ancient trees, their branches interwoven to form a natural barrier. The trees were unlike any Penelope had seen before—their bark shimmered faintly with magic, and the leaves seemed to hum with energy.

At the center of the circle was a stone pedestal, and around it stood five figures, tall and graceful, their forms blending with the trees. These were not ordinary beings—these were the Guardians of the Forest, the ancient protectors that Penelope had heard whispers of but had never seen.

Penelope's breath caught in her throat. "The Guardians..."

The Guardians turned as one to face Penelope and Jasper, their eyes glowing softly with an ancient wisdom. They were tall and ethereal, their bodies composed of a mixture of bark, leaves, and stone, with faint glimmers of light running through them. Each Guardian seemed to embody a different aspect of the forest—one was made of flowing water, another of wind, another of stone, and the remaining two were formed of fire and earth. Together, they represented the elements that sustained the forest's magic.

One of the Guardians stepped forward, their voice a soft, melodic echo. "Welcome, Penelope Pine. We have been waiting for you."

Penelope swallowed, her heart pounding in her chest. "You know who I am?"

The Guardian nodded. "Yes. The forest speaks your name, and the wind carries your story. You are the one who seeks the Lumen Blossom, but you are also here for something greater. The forest is in danger, and only you can save it."

Penelope glanced at Jasper, her mind racing. "What kind of danger? Is it the shadow I've been seeing?"

Another Guardian, whose body was made of flowing water, stepped forward, their voice like the rushing of a stream. "The shadow is part of the danger, but it is only the beginning. The forest's life force is fading. The balance between the elements is weakening, and if it is not restored, the forest will fall into darkness."

Penelope felt a chill run down her spine. "How can I help? What do I need to do?"

The Guardian made of stone stepped forward, their voice deep and resonant, like the rumbling of the earth. "There is an ancient riddle, passed down through the ages. It is the key to restoring balance and protecting the life force of the forest. But only one who understands the forest's magic can solve it."

Jasper raised an eyebrow. "A riddle? I've never been great with riddles."

The Guardian of wind, whose body shimmered with the same energy as the wind crystal Penelope carried, spoke next. "This riddle is not just a test of knowledge—it is a test of the heart. You must use all that you have learned, all that you have experienced, to find the answer."

Penelope took a deep breath, her mind focused. She had come so far, learned so much from the forest, the wind, and the creatures she had met. Whatever this riddle was, she knew it would test everything she had learned on her journey.

"Tell me the riddle," Penelope said, her voice steady. "I'll do my best to solve it."

The Guardians moved closer, forming a protective circle around the stone pedestal at the center of the clearing. The Guardian of fire, their form glowing with a faint, warm light, spoke in a voice that crackled like flames.

"Here is the riddle:
I am born in silence, yet I sing.
I am invisible, yet I am felt.
I am constant, yet I change.
What am I?"

Penelope's mind raced as she repeated the riddle in her head.

Born in silence... yet I sing. Invisible... yet I am felt. Constant... yet I change.

She closed her eyes, thinking back to all she had learned from the forest. The elements, the wind, the balance of nature—it all swirled in her mind, forming a picture of the answer.

"The wind," Penelope whispered, her eyes snapping open. "It's the wind."

The Guardians remained silent, watching her closely.

Penelope stepped forward, her heart pounding. "The wind is born in silence, but it sings as it moves through the trees. It's invisible, but you can feel it on your skin. And though it's constant, always present, it changes—sometimes it's a breeze, sometimes a storm. The answer is the wind."

For a moment, there was no sound but the rustling of the leaves. Then, slowly, the Guardians nodded, their glowing eyes filled with approval.

"You are correct," the Guardian of wind said softly, their voice like a gentle breeze. "The wind is the key to the balance of the forest. You have passed the test."

Penelope let out a breath she hadn't realized she was holding, relief flooding through her.

The Guardian of earth, their voice strong and steady, spoke again. "You have proven yourself worthy, Penelope Pine. The balance of the forest depends on the harmony of the elements, and you have shown that you understand the importance of that balance. But there is still more to be done."

The Guardian of fire stepped forward, their eyes glowing with intensity. "The Lumen Blossom is the final piece of the puzzle. Its power can restore the life force of the forest and banish the shadow once and for all. But beware—the shadow is close, and it will not let you take the blossom without a fight."

Penelope nodded, her resolve hardening. "I'm ready. I'll do whatever it takes to save the forest."

The Guardians moved aside, revealing a path that led deeper into the forest. The magic compass in Penelope's hand glowed brightly, its needle pointing directly down the path. The way to the Lumen Blossom was clear now, but the danger had never been greater.

"Go with the forest's blessing," the Guardian of water said, their voice soft and soothing. "And remember—you are not alone. The elements are with you, and the wind will guide your way."

With one final nod to the Guardians, Penelope and Jasper set off down the path, the weight of the forest's fate resting on their shoulders. The riddle had tested her understanding, but the real challenge was yet to come. The shadow was waiting, and Penelope knew that the battle ahead would be the hardest one yet.

But she was ready.

With the power of the elements at her side and the knowledge that she had gained from the Guardians, Penelope walked with determination, her heart filled with hope. The journey was nearing its end, but her adventure was far from over.

Chapter 29: The Stolen Star

Penelope and Jasper had barely left the clearing where the Guardians of the Forest had tested her when the forest began to change once again. The trees, bathed in the soft golden light of the late afternoon, suddenly seemed darker, their shadows lengthening unnaturally. The air was cooler, and an eerie silence settled over the forest as if the very magic that sustained it was wavering.

"What's happening?" Jasper asked, his voice tinged with nervousness.

Penelope glanced at the sky, her heart skipping a beat. The sun was beginning to set, but something was wrong. The sky, which should have been transitioning into twilight, was dimming far too quickly, and the stars—those tiny, twinkling beacons that always appeared with the night—were missing.

"The stars," Penelope whispered, her eyes wide. "They're not there."

Jasper looked up, his tail flicking in confusion. "But why would the stars disappear?"

Before Penelope could answer, the magic compass in her hand pulsed urgently, its needle spinning wildly as if reacting to the strange shift in the air. Then, from the distant edge of the forest, a brilliant light streaked across the sky—a falling star, brighter than anything Penelope had ever seen. The star plummeted toward the farthest reaches of the forest, disappearing beyond the treetops in a burst of golden light.

Penelope's heart pounded. She had seen shooting stars before, but this was different. The light was too bright, too close, and the forest seemed to tremble in its wake.

"We have to go after it," Penelope said, her voice firm. "That star wasn't supposed to fall."

Jasper's eyes widened. "Do you think it's connected to the forest's magic? The Guardians didn't mention anything about falling stars."

Penelope nodded. "I think it's more than that. The stars disappearing... it has to be connected to the balance of the forest. If we don't fix it, nightfall might disappear forever."

Jasper's tail twitched nervously, but he nodded in agreement. "Then we better hurry. We don't have much time."

With the compass still glowing faintly in her hand, Penelope sprinted through the forest, following the path that the fallen star had blazed through the sky. The trees blurred past her as she ran, her heart pounding with urgency. The sky was growing darker by the minute, and with no stars to light the way, the forest felt more ominous than ever.

As they neared the edge of the forest, Penelope saw a strange light flickering between the trees—golden and warm, like the light of the fallen star. She pushed forward, her feet moving faster until she burst into a small, open glade. There, at the center of the clearing, was the fallen star.

It was beautiful—small and glowing, its light casting soft shadows across the ground. But as Penelope stepped closer, she saw that the star wasn't alone. Standing beside it was a tall figure, cloaked in shadow, their face obscured by darkness. The figure held the star in one hand, and in the other, they gripped a long, gnarled staff that pulsed with dark energy.

"The shadow," Penelope whispered, her heart racing.

Jasper's ears flattened, his voice barely a whisper. "That's the thing from your visions, isn't it?"

Penelope nodded slowly, her eyes fixed on the shadowy figure. She had seen this creature before, in her dreams and in the reflections of the Mirror of Illusions. It had been watching her, waiting for this moment.

The shadow turned toward Penelope, and though its face was hidden, she could feel its gaze on her, cold and unyielding. "You've come for the star," the figure said, its voice low and rumbling, like the wind howling through a cave. "But this star belongs to me now. It is the key to ending the night, and with it, the balance of the forest will fall."

Penelope's hands clenched into fists. "You can't do that! The night is part of the forest's magic. Without it, everything will collapse."

The shadow chuckled darkly, its grip tightening on the star. "That is precisely the point. The forest has grown too strong, too reliant on its precious balance. But without the night, there can be no stars, no magic to sustain it. And when the light fades, the forest will fall into shadow."

Penelope's heart raced. The shadow wanted to destroy the forest by erasing the night. Without the stars, without the cycle of day and night, the magic of the forest would fade, and everything would fall into darkness.

"You won't win," Penelope said, her voice trembling with anger. "I'll stop you."

The shadow tilted its head, as if amused by her defiance. "You are brave, child, but you are only one. You cannot fight the forces that have been at play for centuries."

But Penelope wasn't alone. She had the Guardians' blessing, the magic compass, and the wind crystal, along with everything she had learned about the forest's magic. She had come too far to let the shadow win.

"I'm not just one," Penelope said, her voice steady. "I have the forest with me."

With that, she reached into her satchel and pulled out the wind crystal. The moment her fingers touched the glowing stone, the wind around her stirred, swirling into a powerful gust. The trees bent with the force of the wind, and the shadow's dark cloak rippled violently in the breeze.

The shadow hissed in frustration, clutching the star tightly, but the wind was relentless, growing stronger by the second. Penelope closed her eyes, letting the wind guide her. She knew what to do. She had learned from the Guardians and the whisper of the wind—everything in the forest was connected, and the wind was her ally.

"Give back the star," Penelope commanded, her voice filled with the power of the wind.

The shadow faltered, its grip on the star loosening as the wind howled around it. The dark energy of the staff flickered, struggling to maintain control. Penelope stepped forward, her hand outstretched.

"You can't take the night from the forest," she said firmly. "The balance will be restored."

With a final, deafening gust, the wind tore the star from the shadow's grasp. The golden light flew through the air, landing safely in Penelope's hands. The star pulsed softly, its warmth spreading through her fingers.

The shadow let out a furious roar, the dark energy swirling around it in a vortex of anger and frustration. But as Penelope held the star, its light grew brighter, and the shadow began to retreat, its form fading into the darkness.

"This isn't over," the shadow hissed, its voice echoing in the wind. "The balance may be restored, but the shadow will always linger."

And with that, the shadow disappeared, leaving only the sound of the wind rustling through the trees.

Penelope let out a breath she hadn't realized she was holding, her heart still racing. She looked down at the star in her hands, its golden light flickering softly.

Jasper stepped forward, his voice filled with awe. "You did it, Penelope. You saved the star."

Penelope smiled, the weight of the moment sinking in. "We did it, Jasper."

But the journey wasn't over yet. She had to return the star to the sky before nightfall disappeared forever. The forest depended on the balance of day and night, and without the stars, the magic that sustained it would fade.

With the star in her hands, Penelope and Jasper hurried back through the forest, racing against the setting sun. The sky was growing darker, and the air felt heavy with anticipation. But Penelope knew what to do. She had learned from the Guardians that every part of the forest was connected, and now, she would restore that connection.

As they reached the highest peak in the forest, Penelope stood at the edge of the cliff, the fallen star glowing brightly in her hands. She looked up at the dark sky, where the stars should have been twinkling, and whispered a soft prayer to the forest.

"Let the balance be restored."

With a deep breath, Penelope released the star. It flew upward, soaring into the sky, its light growing brighter as it rejoined the stars above. The moment the star returned to its place, the sky came alive with twinkling lights, the stars sparkling like jewels against the dark canvas of night.

The forest sighed in relief, the balance restored, and Penelope smiled as the magic of the forest pulsed gently around her.

"You did it," Jasper whispered. "The stars are back."

Penelope nodded, her heart filled with peace. "The balance is restored, but the shadow is still out there. We have to stay vigilant."

Jasper looked up at the sky, his eyes filled with wonder. "For now, though, we've saved the night."

With the stars twinkling above and the nightfall safely restored, Penelope and Jasper knew that their adventure wasn't over yet. But for now, the forest was at peace, and the magic that sustained it would continue to shine.

Chapter 30: The Eternal Flame

The stars twinkled brightly above the forest, their light restored after Penelope had returned the fallen star to the sky. The forest breathed with life again, the balance of day and night once more in harmony. But as Penelope and Jasper continued their journey, the magic compass pulsed with renewed urgency, its needle pointing toward an unknown destination deeper in the heart of the woods.

Penelope felt a sense of peace after saving the night, but she knew the shadow wasn't gone for good. The balance was fragile, and the magic that sustained the forest was still under threat. With the compass guiding them forward, they followed a narrow, winding path through the trees until the air grew warmer, and a faint glow appeared on the horizon.

Jasper, perched on Penelope's shoulder, narrowed his eyes. "Do you see that? It looks like a fire, but it's... different."

Penelope nodded, her curiosity piqued. "It's not smoke—just light. Let's get closer."

As they approached, the forest opened up into a vast, circular clearing, and at its center stood something extraordinary. A flame, glowing softly with a golden light, burned steadily atop a stone pedestal. It was unlike any fire Penelope had ever seen—its light was warm and comforting, but there was no heat, no crackling of wood. The flame flickered gently, casting long shadows across the clearing.

But something was wrong. The flame, though still burning, seemed weak. Its light was dimming, and Penelope could sense that it was struggling to stay alight.

"The Eternal Flame," Penelope whispered, awe in her voice. "I've read about it in the Lost Library. It's said to have burned for centuries, protecting the forest's magic."

Jasper hopped down, his nose twitching. "But it's fading. What's causing it to weaken?"

Penelope approached the pedestal cautiously, feeling the warmth of the flame wrap around her like a gentle embrace. She reached out toward the fire, but as her fingers drew near, the flame flickered violently, as if resisting her touch.

"Something's wrong," Penelope said, frowning. "The flame is struggling to stay alive. Its power is fading."

Jasper's ears twitched. "Maybe the shadow had something to do with it. If the shadow wants to destroy the forest's balance, weakening the Eternal Flame would make sense."

Penelope nodded. "We need to find the source of its power. If we don't rekindle the flame, the forest's magic could disappear for good."

As they circled the pedestal, Penelope noticed an inscription carved into the stone, worn and weathered by time:

"The flame of eternity burns with the strength of the forest's heart. Seek the source to reignite the light."

Penelope's heart skipped a beat. The flame's power was connected to the very heart of the forest, the life force that sustained everything—the same life force the Guardians of Eldergreen had told her about.

"The forest's heart," Penelope murmured. "That must be what powers the flame."

Jasper looked up at her, his eyes wide with realization. "But where is the heart of the forest? We've been all over, and we've never seen anything like that."

Penelope thought back to everything she had learned on her journey—the life force, the balance of the elements, the wind crystal, and the Guardians' warning. The forest's heart wasn't a physical place. It was the magic that connected everything, and it flowed through the elements themselves—earth, air, water, fire, and spirit.

"We need to rekindle the flame using the elements," Penelope said suddenly. "The heart of the forest is in everything—the wind, the trees, the rivers. If we can channel the elements into the flame, we can reignite it."

Jasper tilted his head. "How do we do that? We don't have control over the elements."

Penelope reached into her satchel and pulled out the wind crystal, the same one she had used to restore balance after the star had fallen. It glowed faintly in her hand, its energy pulsing with the same gentle rhythm as the wind itself.

"We have the wind," Penelope said softly. "And I think we can call on the others."

Penelope stood before the fading flame, holding the wind crystal in her hand. She closed her eyes and focused on the connection she had felt throughout her journey—the whisper of the wind, the strength of the earth, the flow of water, the warmth of fire. They were all connected, part of the same life force that sustained the forest.

Taking a deep breath, she raised the wind crystal and whispered, "Let the elements restore what is fading. Let the heart of the forest burn bright again."

The moment she spoke, the wind stirred around her, swirling gently through the clearing. The wind crystal glowed brighter, and Penelope felt the breeze carrying with it the magic of the air. The flame flickered, its light growing slightly stronger, but it wasn't enough.

Jasper, realizing what needed to happen, nodded toward a small stream nearby. "The water's next, Penelope. The flame needs it."

Penelope stepped toward the stream and cupped her hands, collecting the cool water. She carried it back to the flame and let a few drops fall into the fire. As the water touched the flame, it hissed softly, but instead of extinguishing it, the flame absorbed the water, its light growing a little brighter.

"Earth and fire," Penelope said, glancing at the ground beneath her feet and the flame itself.

Kneeling, she pressed her hand against the earth, feeling its steady pulse. She whispered a soft prayer to the earth, asking for its strength, and as she stood, she touched the flame with her fingertips, feeling its warmth.

The fire roared softly, its light flaring as it absorbed the strength of the earth and the fire within itself. The flame, once weak and flickering, grew taller, its light casting golden rays across the clearing. But Penelope knew it still needed something more—the spirit of the forest, the unseen magic that connected everything.

Penelope closed her eyes, reaching deep within herself. She had learned so much from the forest, from the Guardians, and from the wind. She had become part of the forest's story, and now she understood that the flame's final strength had to come from her own spirit.

"The balance is restored," she whispered, her voice filled with conviction. "Let the forest's heart burn bright."

A soft, warm glow emanated from Penelope's chest as she opened her eyes. Her connection to the forest—her spirit—flowed into the flame, and with a final surge of magic, the Eternal Flame flared to life, burning brighter than it had in centuries. The light was warm and steady, its golden rays casting a peaceful glow over the forest.

Penelope stepped back, her heart filled with relief. "We did it."

Jasper grinned, his eyes reflecting the flame's glow. "You did it, Penelope. The flame's alive again."

The forest sighed with relief, the balance of its magic restored. The Eternal Flame, once fading and weak, now burned as it had for centuries, protecting the heart of the forest and ensuring its magic would continue to flow.

As Penelope and Jasper stood before the rekindled flame, they knew that the journey wasn't over. The shadow was still out there, waiting, and the final battle for the forest's future was fast approaching.

But with the Eternal Flame burning bright and the balance restored, Penelope felt stronger than ever.

The magic of the forest was with her, and she was ready for whatever came next.

Chapter 31: The Final Trial

With the Eternal Flame rekindled and the balance of the forest restored, Penelope felt a renewed sense of purpose. The magic of the forest pulsed around her, stronger than ever, but a lingering tension hung in the air. She knew the shadow that had been haunting her journey was still out there, waiting for its chance to strike. The final test was near, and the magic compass glowed faintly in her hand, its needle pointing toward the last challenge—the Final Trial.

As Penelope and Jasper followed the compass deeper into the forest, the trees began to change. The once-familiar path gave way to dense fog, and the air grew heavy with an unsettling stillness. The light from the Eternal Flame flickered faintly in the distance, but it was not enough to dispel the growing shadows around them.

"This feels different," Jasper said, his ears flattening against his head. "Like the forest is... shifting."

Penelope nodded, her grip tightening on the compass. "It's the final test. The Guardians warned me there would be a challenge before I could reach the Lumen Blossom."

As they pressed forward, the fog thickened, and soon, they found themselves standing before a towering wall of mirrors, each one reflecting Penelope and Jasper in strange, distorted forms. The mirrors stretched out in all directions, creating a labyrinth of glass and reflections. Penelope could see dozens of versions of herself, each reflection flickering in and out of focus, like fragments of a dream.

"The Labyrinth of Mirrors," Penelope whispered, remembering the stories she had read in the Lost Library. "It's said to be the final test of anyone who seeks the Lumen Blossom. You can't trust what you see in here."

Jasper shifted nervously on her shoulder. "So, it's all illusions?"

Penelope nodded. "Illusions meant to confuse and trick you. But this isn't just a test of finding the way out. It's about trusting yourself—about knowing which path is the right one, even when everything around you says otherwise."

Taking a deep breath, Penelope stepped into the labyrinth, the cool surface of the mirrors reflecting the pale light of the fog. The moment she crossed the threshold, the world around her seemed to shift. The reflections in the mirrors grew sharper, more vivid, and she could see her own face staring back at her from every direction.

The compass in her hand pulsed weakly, its needle spinning wildly as if it were unsure of where to point. Penelope frowned—this was the first time the compass had failed her. She realized that this was part of the test. In the labyrinth of mirrors, she couldn't rely on the compass or her usual tools. She had to rely on herself.

"Stay close, Jasper," Penelope said softly. "We have to be careful."

They moved cautiously through the labyrinth, each step bringing new reflections and illusions. Some mirrors showed Penelope as she was—determined and confident, her eyes fixed on the path ahead. But others showed her distorted, filled with doubt, her reflection flickering with hesitation. Some mirrors reflected dark versions of herself, shadowed and uncertain, as if her fears and insecurities were manifesting before her.

Jasper glanced nervously at one of the mirrors. "Penelope, look—your reflection. It's... changing."

Penelope turned and saw what Jasper meant. The mirror in front of her didn't just reflect her image—it showed her making different choices. In one reflection, she saw herself walking away from the labyrinth, abandoning the quest altogether. In another, she saw herself lost and confused, trapped forever in the maze. And in a third, she stood victorious, holding the Lumen Blossom in her hands, but with an expression of sadness as if something important had been lost along the way.

"These mirrors..." Penelope whispered, her heart pounding. "They're showing me different versions of what could happen. But none of them feel right."

Jasper frowned. "So how do we know which path to take?"

Penelope closed her eyes, focusing on the lessons she had learned throughout her journey. The Guardians, the wind, the Eternal Flame—they had all taught her that the forest's magic wasn't just about seeing with her eyes. It was about trusting her instincts, her heart. The mirrors reflected her doubts and fears, but she had to look beyond them.

"I have to trust myself," Penelope said firmly, opening her eyes. "The mirrors are trying to confuse me, but I know the way."

With renewed determination, Penelope pressed forward, ignoring the mirrors that showed her lost or defeated. She focused on the path ahead, letting her instincts guide her through the maze. As they moved deeper into the labyrinth, the illusions grew stronger. Some mirrors showed her being chased by shadows, others reflected moments of doubt from her past—times when she had hesitated, questioned herself, or felt unsure of her abilities.

But Penelope knew better now. She wasn't the same girl who had started this journey. She had grown, learned to listen to the magic of the forest, and faced her fears head-on. The mirrors were only illusions, and she wouldn't let them control her.

At last, they reached the heart of the labyrinth—a vast, open space surrounded by towering mirrors. In the center of the room stood a single mirror, taller and more elaborate than the rest. Its frame was carved with intricate designs, and its surface shimmered with a strange, otherworldly light.

Penelope approached cautiously, her reflection clear and sharp in the mirror's surface. But as she drew closer, the reflection shifted, and she saw something unexpected. Standing beside her reflection was the shadow—the same figure that had haunted her journey, the dark presence she had confronted when she returned the star to the sky.

The shadow was no longer an indistinct form. Now, it was clearer, more defined—a dark version of Penelope herself, her face twisted with doubt and fear.

The shadow spoke, its voice cold and low. "You can't win, Penelope. You're not strong enough to face what's coming."

Penelope's heart pounded, but she didn't back down. "You're just an illusion. You don't control me."

The shadow sneered. "I am your fear, your doubt, the part of you that questions every choice you've made. You think you're ready for what lies ahead, but you're not. The Lumen Blossom will destroy you, just like it has destroyed others before you."

Penelope felt a chill run down her spine, but she held her ground. She had faced her doubts before, and she had learned that the only way to move forward was to trust herself.

"You don't scare me," Penelope said firmly. "I know who I am. I've come this far because I believe in myself, and I'm not going to let fear stop me now."

The shadow's form flickered, its confidence wavering. "You'll fail."

"No," Penelope said, stepping closer to the mirror. "I won't."

With those words, the shadow faded, disappearing into the glass as if it had never been there. The mirror shimmered and shifted, revealing a path leading out of the labyrinth—a path that led to a bright, glowing light in the distance.

Penelope turned to Jasper, her heart filled with determination. "The final test is over. We're ready."

Jasper grinned, his tail flicking with excitement. "You did it, Penelope. You passed the test."

As they walked toward the glowing light, Penelope felt a sense of peace wash over her. The labyrinth of mirrors had tested her, forcing her to confront her fears and doubts, but she had emerged stronger. The light ahead was bright and warm, and she knew that it would lead her to the Lumen Blossom.

With the final trial behind her, Penelope stepped out of the labyrinth and into the next chapter of her journey—ready to face whatever challenges lay ahead with courage and hope.

Chapter 32: The Discovery of the Lumen Blossom

After passing the Final Trial in the labyrinth of mirrors and illusions, Penelope had proven her strength, her courage, and her ability to trust herself. Every lesson the forest had taught her—every creature she had met, every riddle she had solved—had led her to this moment. And now, with the shadow defeated and the balance of the forest restored, one final task remained: finding the Lumen Blossom.

The Lumen Blossom was more than just a legendary flower. It was the heart of the forest's magic, the key to its renewal and protection. Penelope had seen glimpses of it throughout her journey—through the whispers of the wind, the riddles of the Guardians, and the visions in the Mirror of Illusions. But the time had come to see the Blossom with her own eyes.

The magic compass, which had guided her through every challenge, now pulsed steadily in her hand, its needle pointing toward the heart of the forest. The forest around her seemed to hold its breath, as if it knew that the moment of discovery was near.

"Are you ready?" Jasper asked, his small voice filled with excitement and a little bit of awe.

Penelope smiled, her heart racing. "I've never been more ready."

With each step, the air grew lighter, more vibrant, as if the very essence of the forest was guiding her. The trees that surrounded her were taller and more ancient, their bark shimmering faintly with magic. Flowers bloomed along the path, their petals glowing with soft, radiant light. The wind rustled through the leaves, carrying with it a gentle hum, a melody that seemed to come from the very soul of the forest.

After a short walk through this enchanted part of the woods, Penelope reached a secluded clearing, bathed in golden sunlight. At the center of the clearing was a small hill, covered in soft grass and surrounded by a circle of trees whose branches formed a natural canopy overhead. And there, at the top of the hill, stood the Lumen Blossom.

Penelope's breath caught in her throat. The flower was more beautiful than anything she had imagined. Its petals glowed with a soft, ethereal light, their colors shifting from pale gold to deep violet, like the colors of a sunset. The flower's delicate leaves shimmered, and the air around it seemed to pulse with energy, as if the forest itself was alive within the Blossom.

"The Lumen Blossom," Jasper whispered, his eyes wide with wonder. "It's even more magical than I imagined."

Penelope stepped forward, her heart filled with awe. The closer she got to the Blossom, the more she could feel its power—a quiet, steady strength that seemed to connect everything in the forest. The magic of the wind, the trees, the rivers, the animals—it was all here, in the Lumen Blossom's gentle glow.

Kneeling before the flower, Penelope reached out her hand, her fingers trembling slightly. She had come so far to find this Blossom, faced so many challenges and dangers. And now, here it was, within reach.

As her fingers brushed the soft petals, the Lumen Blossom responded. Its light grew brighter, and a soft, warm energy flowed through Penelope's hand, spreading through her body like a wave of calm and peace. The flower's magic wasn't overwhelming or forceful—it was gentle, reassuring, as if it recognized her as the one who had earned the right to protect it.

Penelope smiled, her heart filled with a deep sense of purpose. The Lumen Blossom had been found, and its power was now in her hands. The forest would be safe.

But as Penelope stood, holding the Blossom's magic within her, a shadow flickered at the edge of the clearing. Penelope's heart skipped a beat. The shadow—the dark presence she had faced before—was still lingering, still waiting for its moment.

The shadowy figure stepped out from the trees, its form shifting and flickering like smoke. Its voice was cold, echoing through the clearing. "You think you've won, but the forest's magic is fragile. You cannot protect it forever."

Penelope stood her ground, the Lumen Blossom's light glowing brightly in her hands. "The forest's magic isn't fragile. It's strong—stronger than you."

The shadow sneered. "Strong? Perhaps. But magic can be twisted, corrupted. And I will be waiting, always lurking in the darkness."

Penelope felt the Blossom's warmth surge through her, filling her with confidence. "You may try to destroy the forest, but you'll never win. The Lumen Blossom is a symbol of hope, of life, and as long as it blooms, the forest will thrive."

The shadow let out a low, angry hiss, but it couldn't approach the Blossom. The light was too strong, too pure. With one final glare, the shadow retreated into the darkness, its form fading into the forest.

Penelope let out a breath of relief. The shadow was gone, for now, but she knew it would always be out there, waiting for a moment of weakness. But the Lumen Blossom's magic would protect the forest, and Penelope had proven that she was more than capable of protecting it, too.

With the shadow gone and the Lumen Blossom glowing brightly in her hands, Penelope turned to Jasper, her eyes shining with excitement. "We did it."

Jasper grinned. "You did it, Penelope. The forest is safe."

As they stood in the clearing, the sun dipped lower in the sky, casting a golden light over the forest. Penelope felt a deep sense of peace. She had found the Lumen Blossom, restored the balance of the forest, and proven that the magic within her was just as strong as the magic of the forest itself.

The adventure had changed her—made her stronger, more confident, and more connected to the world around her. And now, as she looked at the Lumen Blossom's soft glow, she knew that the magic of the forest would always be with her, no matter where she went.

Chapter 33: Home Again

The forest was alive with light and color as Penelope and Jasper made their way back along the familiar paths. The air felt lighter, the wind hummed with warmth, and the trees themselves seemed to sway in gratitude for all she had done. The Lumen Blossom, its soft glow radiating from her satchel, was proof of their victory. The forest was safe, its balance restored, and the shadow that had threatened its magic had been defeated.

But as they neared the edge of the forest, a quiet sense of peace washed over Penelope. She had been through so much—dangerous creatures, ancient riddles, magical trials—and yet, the adventure had taught her something far more valuable than she could have imagined. The forest was full of magic, yes, but so was the world beyond it.

As the trees thinned, revealing the open fields near her home, Penelope stopped for a moment, turning to look back at the forest. She felt the weight of everything that had happened settle on her shoulders, but not in a heavy way. It was more like a comforting warmth, a reminder that she had faced challenges she never thought possible and had come out stronger.

Jasper, perched on her shoulder, broke the silence. "It feels different, doesn't it? Everything looks the same, but... it's not."

Penelope smiled softly. "You're right. I feel different, too. I'm not the same girl who first wandered into the forest."

The adventure had changed her in ways she couldn't fully explain. She had discovered the strength within herself, learned to trust her instincts, and seen the world through the eyes of the forest's magic. She was no longer just a curious girl exploring the woods—she had become part of the forest's story, and the forest had become part of hers.

Together, they walked the final stretch home, the familiar sight of Penelope's cottage coming into view. It looked just as it had before she had set off on her adventure—modest and cozy, with its thatched roof and garden of wildflowers. But to Penelope, it felt different now, as though it, too, had been touched by the magic of the forest.

As they approached the front door, Penelope hesitated for a moment, a soft smile playing on her lips. "I wonder if anyone will believe me when I tell them everything that happened."

Jasper grinned. "Even if they don't, we know the truth. The forest's magic is real, and we've seen it with our own eyes."

Penelope laughed, her heart light. "You're right. And that's what matters."

She pushed open the door and stepped inside, the familiar scent of home wrapping around her like a warm blanket. The sun was beginning to set, casting a golden glow through the windows, and the world outside was quiet and peaceful. For a moment, Penelope stood still, taking in the simplicity of her surroundings—the worn wooden floorboards, the shelves lined with books, the crackling fireplace.

Everything was just as she had left it, but she saw it with new eyes. There was magic here, too—not the kind that came from enchanted maps or glowing crystals, but the kind that lived in the ordinary moments. The gentle warmth of a hearth, the way the evening sun bathed the room in light, the soft rustling of leaves in the breeze.

"I think I finally understand," Penelope said quietly, her voice thoughtful. "The magic isn't just in the forest. It's everywhere—if we know how to see it."

Jasper tilted his head, his eyes twinkling with curiosity. "Even here? In this little cottage?"

Penelope smiled, a sense of wonder filling her heart. "Especially here. Every part of the world is connected, just like the forest. There's magic in the way the sun rises and sets, in the wind that blows through the trees, in the way the stars come out at night. We just have to notice it."

She walked over to the window and looked out at the fields beyond, the sky painted in shades of orange and pink as the sun dipped below the horizon. The stars would soon appear, twinkling like tiny beacons in the night sky—a reminder of the adventure she had completed, but also of the endless possibilities that still lay ahead.

Penelope felt a deep sense of peace. The adventure had taken her to the farthest reaches of the forest, shown her wonders beyond her wildest dreams, and challenged her in ways she never expected. But now, as she stood in the quiet comfort of her home, she realized that the magic of her journey hadn't ended. It would live on in the way she saw the world, in the choices she made, and in the curiosity that still burned within her.

"I think the world will always be a little more magical now," Penelope said softly.

Jasper nodded, his small paws resting on the windowsill. "And who knows? Maybe there's another adventure waiting for us out there."

Penelope smiled, feeling the truth of his words. "Maybe there is."

As the last rays of sunlight disappeared, Penelope felt a quiet contentment settle over her. The world was filled with magic, not just in the extraordinary, but in the simple, everyday moments that so often went unnoticed. And now, after all she had learned, she knew that she would always be able to find that magic, no matter where she was.

With a soft sigh, Penelope settled into a chair by the fire, Jasper curling up beside her. The glow of the flames flickered across the room, casting soft shadows on the walls, and Penelope knew that this was just the beginning. The forest's magic had changed her, opened her eyes to the wonder all around, and she would carry that magic with her wherever she went.

As she drifted off to sleep, Penelope's heart was filled with gratitude—for the adventure, for the friends she had made along the way, and for the quiet, simple magic of home.

Disclaimer

This is a work of fiction. Names, characters, places, and incidents are either the product of the author's imagination or used in a fictitious manner. Any resemblance to actual persons, living or dead, or actual events is purely coincidental.

The magical creatures, enchanted locations, and extraordinary adventures depicted in this story are meant for entertainment and inspiration. The author does not encourage or endorse attempting any dangerous activities, exploring unknown territories without proper guidance, or believing in fictional concepts presented within these pages.

Readers are encouraged to enjoy this imaginative tale and to let their curiosity flourish, while always remembering that the real world may hold wonders of its own, but it requires caution, safety, and respect for nature and others.

Milton Keynes UK
Ingram Content Group UK Ltd.
UKHW040256181024
449757UK00001B/63